Falling For the Doc
By Neva Bodin

This is a work of fiction. Names, characters, places, and incidents are the products of the author's imagination or are used fictitiously. Any resemblance to actual events, locales, or persons, living or dead, is entirely coincidental.

CHAPTER ONE

An energy spun around her as if a giant whirlwind whooshed through the building, drawing all the air from Allison's lungs. Feeling suddenly weak, she looked for something or someone to hold onto, but she was standing by herself near the edge of the dance floor. Her hand pressed against her fluttering heart. He was one handsome dude.

From clear across the room in this community gathering place—small if it were a New York City ballroom, large for this town of Sage Flats, Wyoming, population 2500—she could feel the chemistry. Her eyes were drawn to him. She was shocked at herself. And not just because she felt the sparks. She had fallen in love with someone already and didn't plan to repeat that mistake for a long time. And certainly not with this beautiful bronze. For that's what he was: a tall, tan, strawberry-blonde-haired sculpture in blue jeans, white western shirt, and white hat. The white hat meant a "good guy" if she remembered her cowboy stories right.

Dazed, she welcomed the loud guffaw of a nearby rancher that ended her trance. That "good guy" was not for her. Chemistry wasn't everything. Recent experience had taught her chemistry wasn't a reliable judge of character at all.

Allison reluctantly turned to gaze at the rest of the dancing crowd—blue jeans, boots, and cowboy hats adorned tall, lean, heavy, and short revelers. They all blended together like the flock of sheep she'd seen on the hillside when she'd first driven her old VW Bug into town five weeks earlier...all except for him. Her glance darted to his side of the room again and refocused on a face much closer as her new friend Penny Parker broke the view.

"Allison! I wondered if you were coming! Good! This is the best place for us to get quickly acquainted with the parents of our students."

Allison pulled her navy blue sweater down over the white skirt covering her slim hips and scanned the room again. Was she the only one not in jeans?

She recognized a few faces from acting as playground guard some mornings when parents dropped the kids off at school. But a lot of kids rode the bus.

Parent-teacher conferences hadn't occurred yet, so she should be grateful for this "Before Fall Roundup" party the small ranching community put together each year after classes started. But her confident teacher persona deserted her as she flicked a glance back at Mr. Cowboy. He stirred up a dust storm in her stomach. She was proud she could think in western vernacular already.

"Here." Penny handed her a plastic champagne flute. "Have a glass of bubbly. It's only punch with ginger ale in it, but they like to pretend it's an upper-class party, hence the fancy plastic. The only other drink you'll see here tonight is beer, and I didn't know if you wanted that."

Allison looked into Penny's face and saw open friendliness. They'd met the first day at school when they attended the new teachers' get-acquainted tea. Penny had already been there a year and was at the tea to mentor a newbie.

The two had clicked and now checked in with each other every day to see how the other was doing in this foreign world of ranching and cowboys. Discovering they were both big-city girls—Penny from St. Louis and Allison from New York—they asked each other how anyone could tell one sheep or one cow from another, and wondered together if they could stand to live thirty or forty miles from any city, surrounded only by red cliffs, blue-green sage, and maize-colored grass. They found the absence of steady traffic unsettling.

They spoke of various reasons for seeking and accepting small-town teaching positions in a culture completely outside their experience, but Allison never gave her real reason. It was too painful. Maybe someday she could share why she had moved halfway across the country to this small town in Wyoming, and whom she was still in love with. Maybe. She hadn't even told her parents the real reason.

The cacophony of guitars, drums, and a keyboard suddenly morphed into a rhythmic synchronized harmony in the corner of the big room. As she opened her mouth to thank Penny for the punch, a large, callused hand at the end of a red-plaid flannel shirtsleeve took the drink from her and handed it back to Penny. A deep voice said, "Can I have this dance, little lady?" Before she could decide, she was firmly whirled out onto the dance floor, jostling with other dancers until she and her partner slipped into some semblance of cooperating in the two-step. Taking her eyes off her feet, she found herself looking at a spot on the man's chest that was even with his armpits. She looked up.

The man was smiling down at her. She guessed him to be at least six foot six. The fresh scent of some kind of deodorant wafted into her nostrils. He had broad shoulders, black hair, and eyes that also appeared black as the room lights were dimmed for the dance. *Must have some Native American in him.*

She'd already met some of the school personnel who were part Native American, not that she could always tell, especially when they had last names like Nelson, and Zarski. She supposed the early trappers and settlers were responsible for much of the mixed heritage in the West, and she found it fascinating. She would have to try and incorporate some of that history into her fifth-grade class.

"My name is Shorty Westhope, and you are...?" He waited for her response, still maintaining his smile.

"Allison White." *How can a tall drink like this guy be called "Shorty"?*

"What's going through that pretty little head of yours?" Shorty twirled her in a full circle and out of another couple's trajectory.

"How come you're called 'Shorty'?" *Man, Allison, you are a brilliant conversationalist. They'll all be wanting you for their kids' teacher.*

"Guess, it's 'cause I'm so short!" he boomed and punctuated it with a roaring laugh.

Just then Allison's heel slid sideways, and like a greased pig she'd seen do once at a carnival, she slipped right out of the man's arms and sprawled onto the floor, doing the splits in the process. She hastily slapped her knees together and pulled her skirt down.

People scattered, then circled, and a chorus of "Are you okay?" queries sailed her way. She sat up stunned, embarrassed, and there he was, his white hat close enough to touch if she wouldn't have needed both her hands to prop herself up.

"I'm Dr. Mac. Are you hurt?" Concerned blue eyes searched her green ones and kicked off an electrical shock that shimmered down from her heart to her ankle, where it seemed to be starting a fire. She moved the injured area and gasped.

"I think I sprained my ankle!" She held her right foot up, inspecting the appendage and wondering why it still appeared normal when it hurt so badly. While she exulted at the luck of his being a doctor, she was mortified at being so clumsy and bringing all this attention on herself.

She began planning how she was going to get to her feet. Suddenly the problem was solved. Dr. Mac scooped her up without even losing his hat, carried her over to a bench beside the wall, and after setting her gently down, knelt in front of her.

"Let me feel your ankle and see if you broke it." He carefully removed her shoe and palpated her limb halfway up to her knee with probing fingers. He began to rotate her ankle and stopped when she immediately yelped, "Ouch!" She felt a warmth in the area he touched that had nothing to do with the injury. Embarrassed, she tried to pull her foot out of his grasp. He let go and looked up at her.

"I think you need an x-ray. It's already starting to swell." Thankfully, most of the onlookers had left to resume their dancing, and the heat in her cheeks was cooling.

"An x-ray!" she squeaked. She deplored being a bother or having done something as stupid as slipping. She looked around for Shorty and noticed him out on the dance floor with someone who looked competent enough to dance without falling over. Tears threatened to ruin her mascara as she squeezed her eyes shut.

"Do you want me to take you?" The voice was Penny's, and her face was swimming there when Allison opened her watery eyes.

"I'll take her," Dr. Mac said, as Allison was nodding at Penny. "You go on and have fun. I'm on call anyway so wasn't planning on staying too long. I'll see she gets to the ER and home safely. You stay and have fun," he repeated and put his hand on Penny's shoulder.

"Well, if you're sure," Penny hesitated, "is that okay with you Allison? Dr. Mac's a good guy and he'll be able to carry you to the car and into the ER, which I couldn't do. And if you get called out before she's done," she turned to the doctor, "just give me a call on my cell, and I'll come get her to take her home."

Sensing Penny's wish to stay, Allison put her own wishes to the back of her mind and nodded. She was afraid a sob would escape if she opened her mouth.

"Okay," Dr. Mac said. "Off we go." He gathered Allison up in his arms again, and while Penny ran ahead and opened his pickup, he carried Allison out across the parking lot and deposited her on the front seat of his truck. The heat and strength in his arms as he'd held her felt like a safe cocoon, something she'd been needing lately.

She briefly noted he had a large, muddy pickup with some sort of cover on the box and thought, this must be how a small-town doctor gets around. Maybe he does house calls. While watching him walk to the driver's side, her ankle caused a sharp intake of breath as her foot made contact with the floor.

The air inside smelled...not fresh exactly, not antiseptic-like which might be expected in a doctor's vehicle, but earthy, or country. *This must be how a country doc's vehicle smells. I like it better than breathing in New York City's odors of asphalt and car fumes.*

He got in behind the steering wheel and they were soon bouncing over the potholes in the parking lot on their way to the hospital. She had to concentrate on holding her foot off the floor, because the first bounce caused her to step down again and she barely swallowed the yell that emerged as a whimper.

The town being small, they reached the ER in under five minutes. Dr. Mac expertly slid her off the truck seat into his arms and headed for the automatic doors labeled "Emergency." Once inside, a short, graying, but smooth-cheeked lady in scrubs hurried toward them.

"Hi, Mac! Who have you got there? Isn't often our county's vet brings his patients to *our* ER!"

CHAPTER TWO

"Hi, my name is Mary, and I'm the nurse who will help you tonight," the gray-haired lady greeted Allison, whose mouth hung open under an accusing stare fixed on *Dr.* Mac. Allison gave Mary a quick glance and resumed her stare.

"You're a *horse* doctor?" she questioned in the same quality of voice she would use on a horse thief. Horse thieves were one of the lowest forms on the western frontier according to the westerns she'd read.

"Now, now," his tone was soothing. "Where should I put her, Mary?" He looked all around the room, turning in a circle with Allison in his arms, making her mouth snap shut as dizziness swirled in her head.

"Bring her this way." The nurse turned down a hallway, and Mac followed.

The place smelled clean and fresh, with no antiseptic or strong odors. The tile floors were shiny, echoing the slap of Mac's cowboy boots. They entered a room where three long narrow carts on wheels were covered with white sheets. Mary pointed at one and Mac deposited Allison on it.

"I'll leave you two to get at it. I'll just be in the waiting room until you're done." He nodded and hastily backed out the door, not holding her scathing stare.

"So...what's the story?" Mary asked.

Allison slid her gaze back to the woman before her.

"He's a veterinary doctor?" she asked again, momentarily forgetting her injury.

"Yes, and a very popular one in these parts—the only one, in fact. He didn't tell you? Now...why did he bring you to our ER?"

Allison's sense of humor returned, albeit mixed with a sense of being plopped down in a foreign world.

"Because I'm not a cow?"

Mary smiled at her, and her face softened with kindness and concern.

"That might be one reason, but there must be another."

"Oh! My ankle. I was dancing at the Before Fall Roundup party in my high heels and my foot slipped. My ankle turned and *Dr.* Mac examined it and thought I needed an x-ray." During this recitation, she noted she was wearing only one shoe and the *animal* doctor must have the other. Or maybe Penny did. Suddenly weary, her ankle's throbbing caught her attention, and her foot was getting cold.

She blinked away tears. "I don't want to be here."

"Most people don't," Mary said. "Now let's get some information from you and I'll call our people doctor." She grinned impishly.

Allison smiled as she sniffed and grabbed a tissue from the box Mary had unobtrusively deposited on a metal stand near her.

Two hours later, x-rayed and examined by a "real" doctor, she was pronounced free to go. Sporting a borrowed pair of crutches and an ankle covered in elastic wrap, she did her best to maintain a cool dignity as she practiced mastering swinging her crutches, then her body, in a forward motion while holding the injured leg off the floor. She used her strongest student-intimidating look on Dr. Mac as she did so and accidentally planted her right crutch on her shoe sitting beside the man's foot. As the shoe and crutch went south, she went north...into his lap.

"Whoa!" he said as if talking to his horse. "I got you!" he added as her shoulder jabbed his chest and her head landed on his shoulder. Crutches banged on the floor as her arms searched for anything solid, and found the muscled bicep on his left arm. The muscle flexed and her fingers tingled. Leveraging to sit upright, she found herself a few inches from his face as she turned her head to look at him. This time Dr. Mac *had* lost his hat. A lock of strawberry-blonde hair hung endearingly down the middle of his forehead. For a few seconds, their gazes locked on each other.

It was a diminutive moment, but very memorable as a static charge sizzled between them. Allison shot up to stand on one leg and reach for the rescued crutches Mary held out to her, while gingerly slipping her foot into the offending shoe now placed in front of her. Luckily, she had worn her one-inch heels instead of the stilettos she owned. She wished she'd worn jeans and cowboy boots as so many others at the dance had done.

"Let's go," she commanded and without looking back, began her halting gate toward the door. She hoped the cold night air would blanch the red from her cheeks and cool the heat in her veins.

"Guess we're gone," she heard Dr. Mac, the animal doctor, say behind her. She spotted his pickup and headed for it, realizing that in all the excitement, she'd left her coat back at the Community Center. A chill from the September night breeze penetrated her sweater and her teeth made a clacking sound. She clenched them together as she stopped by the truck. Mac seemed uncharacteristically silent as he reached around her to open the door. She handed him the crutches, wondering how to hop up and into the passenger seat when strong arms again picked her up and slid her nicely into place.

"Thank you," she murmured with her eyes lowered as she arranged her new walking aides beside her.

"You're welcome."

She stared straight ahead into the night as her rescuer walked around the vehicle and got behind the wheel, closing the door and turning the heater on high. The still-warm air slowly blew her chills away as he drove back to the party. The silence grew loud as they approached the building.

When he stopped, Allison reached for the door handle, and he laid his hand on her arm.

"Wait," he said. His fingers were warm and, she couldn't explain it, but they felt safe and reassuring. *I'm a poor judge of that, so I better stop being whimsical.*

She looked at him then, not sure how to feel or act. Despite her chills moments before, her cheeks were glowing embers.

"We haven't been properly introduced. My name is Ian MacFadden, but everyone calls me Dr. Mac because few know how to pronounce Ian." As he said his name, a slight Scottish brogue crept into the sounds. "Please call me Mac."

His accent charmed her, and she stared at his profile in the dark pickup cab. Was he as innocent and wholesome as he appeared? Did he deserve to wear a white hat? *I'm jaded. I can't trust my own judgment anymore.*

"And you are?" he prompted.

She stared at him, still lost in thought. He tilted his head toward her. "Oh! I'm Allison White, the new teacher for fifth grade."

"Pleased to make your acquaintance, Ms. Allison White. Would you like to go back into the ball?"

She nodded. He exited and met her as she swung her body around, offering his hand and easing her descent back to the ground to balance on one leg.

As they re-entered the Community Center, nearby dancers paused and turned toward them. "Welcome back, are you okay?" chorused several, and Mac answered for her.

"Just a little sprain. She'll still be able to teach our kids, folks." As he steered her toward a bench, he leaned close and asked, "Want some punch now?" His minty breath tickled her neck and sent shivers down her spine.

She wanted to just get her coat and head back to the little house she'd rented on the edge of town. People still watched her as if they expected her to repeat the previous humiliating scene, so she just nodded and tried to figure out how to sit down gracefully with her painful injury and two crutches. She finally managed to thump down, with her offending ankle sticking out ahead of her and almost tripping a cowgirl hurrying by. She was now a hazard to others as well as herself.

Why did this have to happen? I just wanted a safe job, in a safe place where I could blend in with the cows. Or maybe sheep. Her shoulders slumped as she stared at her lap, glad it was Friday night, and she could sleep in the next day. *Best drink my punch and get home.*

Mac returned with two of the fancy plastic glasses of red punch. The bench creaked as he sat down beside her. She felt dwarfed by him, as she had while dancing with Shorty. *I'm five six and he must be almost a foot taller than me. Do they grow all of them big out here? What do they eat?*

CHAPTER THREE

She poured the punch down her dry throat and turned to the animal doctor, as she now thought of him.

"I'm going to excuse myself and go home. I thank you for your assistance tonight, you were very kind." She put one hand on the bench and grabbed the crutches with the other, concentrating on rising gracefully at first, then trying to find a way to just rise at all.

What a disastrous night. Why can't life be smooth sailing? That's what she'd planned when moving to this way-out-west town. Slow, sweet, and safe. Irritated with life, she glanced at the hand being held in front of her, large and secure looking.

"Thanks," she murmured as she grabbed the hand and pulled herself to her...foot. She had a momentary vision of a flamingo as she kept the offending leg raised. She glanced at Mac, who had the temerity to smile.

"How will you drive your car with your right ankle hurting? Let me drive you home, and we'll figure out a way to pick up your car tomorrow."

Her heart sank at his words. How could she drive? It would hurt to put pressure on the accelerator or the brake even though she had an automatic. She'd sprained the wrong ankle. Couldn't she do anything right?

"I'm so sorry for all the trouble I'm causing you." She looked up at him with a frown and a wrinkle between her brows. "If you're sure you have the time, I guess I have to take you up on your offer," she added, a bit ungraciously. "Can you please retrieve my coat from the coat room? It's brown with a fur collar."

"My pleasure," his voice rumbled with just a hint of Scottish burr in the "r."

Meeting her halfway to the exit, he assisted the maneuvering of crutches, arms, and coat so all ended up in appropriate places, then held the door as she exited into the nippy, fall air. Her right foot was feeling heavier by the minute. She blinked away the sudden moisture gathering in her eyes. She would be so glad when this night ended.

Mac lifted her into his high pickup and ten minutes later drove her as close to the door of her aging frame rental as possible. Lifting her out of the pickup, he stayed close as she found a rhythm in swinging the crutches and then her body as she made her way across the driveway. Thankfully, there were only two low-rise stairs to the entrance, and he waited while she retrieved her key from her coat pocket and opened the door which led directly into the kitchen of the small house. He marveled she didn't have a purse, and that she maneuvered on heels with her crutches. Magnificent balance, he thought. Then he remembered her fall and smiled.

She turned to him and said, "Thank you again, Dr. Mac, for all you've done; you were a big help. I hope I can return the favor sometime." Her eyes widened and she opened her mouth in an "O" shape before hastily adding, "I mean, another favor, not this particular favor. I wouldn't want you to sprain your ankle, or...or anything bad." Her gaze dropped to the ground.

He watched the consternation play across her face and took pity. He touched her arm and said, "I understand. It's okay. Please, just call me Mac. Maybe you can make me a home-cooked meal sometime. I'm glad I was there to help. That's what people do in this little town—help each other out. Who knows, I might need your help with my son, Paddy; he's in your class. You get some rest, and I'll see you sometime tomorrow when I get your car home for you. Goodnight, sleep tight, don't let the bedbugs bite," he chided, keeping his smile to lighten the moment.

One of his hands rose like a balloon filled with helium toward her face to brush a feathery touch across her cheek as her eyes found his. He hadn't planned that and didn't know what had come over his hand. He thought he had control of his appendages, but apparently not tonight. He backed away and touched his hat as he turned toward his vehicle. Strange, but he felt as if he was leaving something important behind. He heard her close the house door as he opened the door of his truck.

And then he heard her scream.

CHAPTER FOUR

Mac left his pickup door ajar to run the short distance back and shove the house door open, nearly wrenching the doorknob loose as he barged in. Allison lay on the floor on one hip, propping her upper torso upright with her hands, crutches lying beside her. She was staring at the other end of the room. Focused only on her when he entered, he raised his gaze to where hers was trained and saw a tall, well-built man in gray slacks, light blue shirt, and dark blue sports jacket. The man started forward with his right hand outstretched.

"Hi, my name's Jack Corbel. I'm Allie's fiancé." He strode toward Mac as he delivered this bombshell, and Mac automatically reached to shake the man's hand. "I'm afraid I scared Allie with my surprise," the man continued smoothly, neither voice nor face indicating remorse nor concern that "Allie" was still on the floor.

Jack looked down at Allie. "What'd you do, Allie? Did I surprise you that much or did you trip over your lower lip? Allie has a habit of pouting," Jack looked back at Mac. "When she doesn't get her way that lower lip starts to sag. Kind of cute, but not very attractive if you know what I mean. Ever had a woman like that?"

"Ian MacFadden," Mac said, ignoring Jack's question after he quickly dropped the man's hand. He turned and leaned over Allison, putting his large hands under her arms and lifting her as if she were no heavier than a small child. As she perched on her good leg, he bent down for her crutches, handing them to her as he straightened. The able fiancé hadn't moved.

Incredulous that a fiancé would belittle Allison in that manner, Mac felt a sudden need to defend her. His hands fisted and he stiffened his arms to keep them at his sides.

"Allison?" he queried, "is he your fiancé?" He rolled his "r" through gritted teeth.

"No!" she spat out as she stared at Jack.

"Yes!" Jack took a step toward Allison. "You know we're engaged, Sweetheart. You hurt my feelings when you left without telling me why. But I forgive you. I didn't think we'd ended our engagement. I gave you enough time to cool off if you were upset for some reason, and I've come to take you home. I crawled in through a back window so I could surprise you when you came back from wherever you were." He turned again to Mac.

"Thank you for your help. We'll get this ironed out and say hello if we see you tomorrow." He walked to the door and opened it, waiting for Mac to walk out.

Mac studied their faces, unsure what his role was. He wanted to get Allison away from this smooth-talking city-slicker but figured their short acquaintance gave him no rights. And what if she really was engaged to him, and she had left, testing if this guy would follow her and prove his love?

"Allison? Will you be all right?" Mac noted her stare at the floor.

"Of course, she'll be all right! We're good together. I'm her knight in shining armor!" Jack waved an arm toward the open door while holding Mac's stare.

Perplexed, Mac turned and headed out.

Mac went over the scene repeatedly as he drove back to his clinic and ranchette a half-mile out in the country on the other side of town. Was Allison in trouble? And was he a fool to even wonder if he should get involved?

Drawing on a practice he'd been neglecting of late, he stood on his front step and looked up at the inky sky, void of stars but heavy with blue-black clouds. *God, can you protect her? If she needs it of course. I am drawn to her. You saw that, didn't you? But can I trust her? Is she worth worrying about? I mean, I know she's your child and because of that I should be concerned for her... but is she someone I should worry about? Care about? Man, I'm confused here. Life is supposed to be simple for*

Paddy and me. Can't we keep it that way? It hurts too much to love and lose. You remember, don't you? I was mad at you for a long time.

Not sensing an immediate answer but feeling reassured he wasn't alone in his confusion, he paused a moment longer as his unease lessened, then walked into his house. His housekeeper, in her sixties and widowed, lived with him and his son and doubled as his sitter when he was making calls or gone for any reason. Both she and Patrick were asleep, and the house released only the squeaking sounds of his boots as he walked and the hum of a humidifier in the housekeeper's bedroom. He headed for Paddy's room to reassure himself the current love of his life was okay.

He supposed he'd have to stop calling Patrick "Paddy" one of these days. He'd want his grown-up name. Already the soft vulnerable look of a small boy was becoming the angled face of a growing male child on his way to manhood. He softly smoothed the warm cheek with the back of his finger. *Aw, Catherine, you should see your son now. He's stubborn like me, and beautiful like you. And I miss your being here to share him. And I miss your being here for me.*

He returned to the kitchen and reached for a glass, drawing water from the tap to wash away the lump in his throat. As he did, his cell phone buzzed, and the usual annoyance at a midnight call eased into relief that he would have someone's troubles other than his own to concentrate on for a while.

"Come here, Allie, and sit down. We need to talk." Jack's voice, so oily and smooth, grated like sandpaper across the tight, fragile wire of her emotions.

"I prefer to stand!" But she didn't know how much longer she could. Everything she'd been building the past few weeks in her life seemed ready to topple, including her.

CHAPTER FIVE

Allison's tottering body forced her to accept Jack's invitation to sit down in her own house—a house she had felt safe in before tonight. She leaned her crutches against the table and plopped down on the kitchen chair. She still couldn't force herself to look into the face of a man she'd thought to leave behind when she moved to Wyoming.

"Why are you here?" she asked dully.

"Because I still need you, Allie. You are my salvation. My ace-in-the-hole. You knew that when you left, but you still left. Didn't you know I'd find you when I needed you again?"

Her heartbeat stumbled. What was he talking about? Needed her how? Her love? What else could she give him? What was an ace in a hole?

He reached across the table. "Allie, give me your hand."

She remembered what it was like when she'd first met him, the warmth and thrill of holding that hand had reverberated all the way to her toes. And she remembered how it felt the last time she held it, hard and crushing as she'd yanked hers out of its grip when she'd realized the kind of man she'd given her heart to. She kept her hands squeezed together in her lap.

"What makes you need me now? What have you done that I can fix for you? With your connections, you don't need me!" she shouted, her voice increasing to a crescendo as she talked.

"Allie, calm down. I will always need you. You remember how it used to be, don't you? We love each other. You agreed to marry me. I brought the diamond," his voice turned soft and coaxing. "I knew you didn't mean it when you gave it back. I kept it for you. Only *you* have this hold on me. Let me stay with you for a while. Let's work this out. We were meant for each other."

Allison looked up and saw the pleading look in his eyes, so sincere, so inviting. Her will to hate him began to waffle. His charm and charisma were working again. They radiated from him like heat from the sun. And they worked on anyone he encountered.

Her father, a successful defense lawyer, had become his back-patting supporter immediately upon her bringing him to a family dinner. Her mother had preened and fixed what he declared to be his favorite dishes. Their romance was only three months old when she'd discovered the real Jack, right after accepting the engagement ring.

She'd gone to a fancy New York restaurant with him, wearing the 3-carat diamond, feeling chic and important as various male friends of his also dining there, all impeccably groomed and smelling of expensive aftershave, greeted and complimented him on his gorgeous fiancée as they walked to their reserved table. Her new black dress hugged her curves, and while high in front, draped to a low V in the back, showing her creamy skin peeking through her honey-colored tresses that flowed down her back almost to her waist. She'd felt beautiful and elegant. Her former insecurities and questionable self-esteem had seemed to dissolve. *I'm finally the mature, secure, female I was meant to be. I've arrived.*

She had smiled and nodded her way to their table with Jack's hand on her back. They were dining with two other couples whom she didn't know, and who hadn't yet appeared. But she figured any friends of Jack's would be friends of hers. They had warned they'd be arriving late, and Allie and Jack should go ahead and order without them.

Caviar as an appetizer didn't seem too bad when washed down with a glass of wine. But suddenly her stomach rebelled, causing her to give Jack a wavering smile and excuse herself.

The "powder room" was empty save for two women talking softly in a corner by a mirror. Neither looked her way as Allison glanced at them and ducked into a stall, closed the door, and planned to take deep breaths to hopefully settle her stomach. She heard the name "Jack." She held her breath as she tuned into the voices.

"Did you see his latest when we walked in?" the soft, cultured voice asked. "I wonder what her advantage is."

"I don't know what it could be," the other voice replied. "But knowing Jack, there has to be one. Maybe her daddy's a lawyer and can keep him out of jail. Or maybe a prison guard who'll guard his back if he lands *in* jail!" The two laughed.

"It's a pure waste to have a face and personality like that, and not much between the ears to recommend," the first voice said.

"For sure," the second voice agreed.

Heels clacked as the whoosh of the door announced their departure, and Allison began to breathe again. The deep, stomach-calming breaths she'd planned never happened. Instead, she turned just in time to release the caviar and wine into New York City's sewer system, panting in relief as the nausea lessened.

She rinsed her mouth at the sink by cupping water into her hand, reapplied her lipstick, and wended her way between tables and potted plants to appear at Jack's side. He stood to hold her chair for her, then turned back to their tablemates who had now arrived, not even noticing her pale face and puckered brows.

She placed her napkin in her lap, looked up at the two chattering women sitting across from her, and stifled a sudden gasp. She recognized their voices and faces as the two women in the lavatory. She realized what she'd overheard moments before *was* about *her* Jack. She had told herself all the way to the table it couldn't have been. Her stomach clenched as the truth bit into it.

Afterward, bending to a sixth sense, she'd called a private investigator friend of the family, named Phillip, asking him to do a background check on Jack. What she'd found out had chilled her blood.

She had thanked the good Lord when she'd found a job listing for teachers in Wyoming shortly after the investigator's call. She'd sent the ring back to Jack by registered mail and changed her phone number, making it unlisted.

Luckily, she'd not accepted a new teaching position in New York that would have kept her tied to the area that Fall. She'd met Jack just before the end of the previous school year, and marriage and financial security, enough to stay at home and be his loving wife, seemed in her near future.

Obtaining this teaching position in Wyoming, she thought she'd slipped "out of Dodge," so to speak, and left no tracks. A mistaken notion apparently.

"Allie. I don't think you're listening to me. What's with the crutches anyway?"

Allison cleared her memories to concentrate on the present situation.

"I sprained my ankle at the dance. Dr. Mac—Dr. MacFadden—took me to the ER, and since I couldn't drive, brought me home. He was very nice and went out of his way to take care of me. It was very embarrassing, but all the people were concerned. It's really a nice community here."

She didn't understand why she was babbling or explaining to Jack. She despised her vulnerable feeling in Jack's presence.

Jack spoke again. "How clumsy of you. But then your beauty outshines your imperfections. And I love you enough to overlook the latter. You are my shining star. Life in New York was empty without you. A month of not seeing you about tore me apart, Sweetheart.

"Why did you leave? When I got the ring back, I knew you must have thought I did something wrong, but I couldn't figure out what. It must have been in your mind, 'cause all I've done is love you and treat you like my queen! Whatever got into you, Allie?"

Allison stared at his wide eyes searching hers with all the apparent sincerity of a dog begging for a bone. His hands were palm up and held out to her. His pretty brown eyes with lashes any girl would envy showed such earnestness; again, she knew the old pull. *This must be love, else why would I still want to stroke his face, hold his head, and comfort him? Am I that insecure? That pitiful?*

She forced her eyes to stare at her knees. The pull lessened. She pictured the face of Dr. Mac, openly honest—there, but not intrusive—just looking capable and considerate. She must prevent herself from falling under Jack's spell again. But how?

Why had he followed her, and more importantly, how? She'd instructed her parents to tell no one where she'd gone, leaving their address as her only one and getting a P.O. box in Wyoming. Had they inadvertently betrayed her? Had Jack's "connections" tracked her down?

"I don't want to be engaged to you anymore," she murmured.

"What...what did you say?" Jack's voice sounded incredulous. "How could you not want to be my wife? I can offer you everything, I will take care of you, turn you into the envy of all my friends' and associates' wives! You are very lucky I still want you!"

"But *I* don't want *you*!" Afraid to scream her real reasons, she tried to convince him. "I don't *love* you." Afraid in her heart she understood the kind of person he was and loved him anyway, her words came out sounding weaker than she intended.

"I want you to leave now. I have a new life here, a job to do. Please go back home. We need to end it. *Please.*" She hated the piteous sound to her voice. She was tired and he alarmed her, and she was so afraid she'd lost control of what was happening to her. Tears gathered and spilled, tickling the sides of her nose as they forged a path to her chin.

Jack got up and walked to her side. Kneeling, he looked up into her eyes and said, "Now, Allie, you know better than that. We love each other. You're just overwhelmed. Let me bunk on your couch tonight and we'll talk about it in the morning. You've had a hard night—spraining your ankle, being brought home by a rough cowboy—we'll make plans in the morning. Let me help you into your bedroom."

Allison looked at the handsome face with the dimpled chin. The familiar longing to surrender to his arms raised her hands. The intoxicating feeling of being held while her forehead nestled against his warm neck caused her to lean toward him.

She saw a look of triumph on his face and blinked. What was she doing? With strength of will, she raised her gaze to focus on the old white refrigerator which had kicked in with a rumble and loud purr in the corner of the small kitchen. She straightened her spine and resisted the power of Jack's magnetic field.

Confused and weak, she pushed herself up as Jack rose and put his arms around her, helping her rise and pulling her to him at the same time. She shoved against his chest shouting, "No! Just hand me my crutches!"

"Okay, Darling. We'll talk more in the morning. Get your beauty sleep. I can see you need it." And with that parting shot, Jack grabbed a duffel bag from beside the table and headed for the small bathroom in the hall.

Allison gripped her crutches and maneuvered toward her bedroom across from the bathroom, passing through the living room on the way and wondering how Jack would fit on the short, lumpy couch. The petite rental had two small bedrooms, one of which she used for storage. The place was furnished with furniture from the '50s, had no locks on the windows, and just a deadbolt on the one door that worked. But she'd felt safe and secure...until now.

CHAPTER SIX

The radiant pink and orange sunrise, making the mesas on the eastern horizon dark ochre, failed to catch Mac's attention as he turned the pickup into his driveway. Weary and smelling like barn and antiseptic, he hoped Paddy would be quiet this morning. Mac needed some sleep before he opened the clinic.

He kept his cell phone on, even when he slept. He was on call twenty-four seven. He'd put an ad in a few journals, looking for a partner, but so far no one seemed to want to bury him- or herself out on the lone prairie beside him.

He was pleased he'd delivered a live baby calf for the rancher. A heifer. But the cow had needed a caesarian section and would be sold in the Fall after raising her calf. He knew the way animals were managed, but he always felt sympathy for the ones he treated.

Sometimes he felt too soft-hearted to be a vet. Yet he'd known since he could talk that was what he wanted to be. When, in fourth grade, he'd seen a classmate hitting a pet dog, Mac had a black eye to show his mother as payment for rescuing the mutt. Anyone who abused an animal was as bad as a murderer in his book. That dog had been his confidant until his last year of high school when death from old age took his furry friend.

That was a long time ago, he reminded himself when the memory surfaced, as it often did when he questioned his soft heart. Now he felt old, jaded, and worn, knowing he'd see the crevices of age outlining his eyes this morning. He was only thirty-two but was already wondering if he'd have the energy to keep this lifestyle going into his sixties.

As he brought the truck to a stop and turned off the ignition, the energy to get out and head for the house was missing. Instead, he relished the quiet to let his mind drift to another memory—last night with Allison. Who was Jack, and for that matter, who was Allison? She had seemed so wholesome and uncomplicated when he'd seen her at the dance, taken her to the ER, and brought her home. Then Jack happened. Was she really engaged?

He remembered her face when Jack was talking. She hadn't looked pleased. She'd even seemed fearful. Why did he care? She was an adult, if she had baggage, let her handle it. But, and here was the clincher, he did care. He'd been drawn to her, feeling like a small campfire had kindled near his heart, not unlike when he'd first seen Patrick's mother, something he'd not expected to feel ever again.

Catherine had been gone two years, a victim of a cancerous melanoma. Too much sun when she was young, the doctor had said. And for a long time, the sun was gone from Mac's life after she died, and from Paddy's. Now they were just beginning to have a routine again, to feel connected. Maybe he shouldn't entertain thoughts of another woman this soon. What would that do to Paddy? Too many questions for a tired brain. He needed a shower.

The bright sun was now above the cliffs as he walked into his house and shed his boots and coveralls in the mud room. He'd throw the garment in the washer later; he had another pair if called out again. He washed his arms and hands with lye soap and dried them on a thick, soft towel, one of the luxuries he allowed himself after all the strong soaps and disinfectants he used that chapped his hands.

"Good morning, Regina," he greeted the plump housekeeper as he entered the kitchen.

She turned from stirring the oatmeal to peruse his face and say, "What would you like for breakfast? Apparently, you've been up all night?"

"I have, and oatmeal's fine. I'm going to try a nap after breakfast, so don't want anything too heavy on my stomach anyway. Is Paddy up yet?"

"No, you can wake him if you want. He'll likely be up soon to watch cartoons anyway. His clothes are laid out. I suppose one of these days he'll inform me he's too old at age ten to have me pick out his clothes and he'll start mismatching what he wears all by himself." She chuckled as she turned back to the oatmeal.

"No doubt," he said as he headed for his son's bedroom. His heart squeezed with emotion as always when looking at his son who slept with his mouth open. Two front teeth, looking too large now, but fine teeth for a growing face, shown in the semi-darkness. Mac opened the drapes and began to sing a good morning song.

"Dad! I hate that song!" Patrick's hand flew up to cover his eyes.

Suddenly Mac's voice stopped singing and turned serious. "Paddy," he said as he sat down on the edge of the bed, "what do you think of your new teacher?"

Allison opened her eyes as the room began to lighten. She sensed something not right, then noticed the small dresser she'd wedged against her doorknob before going to bed, and the memory suddenly flooding her mind sent waves of anxiety washing through her. Jack was in her house. And it was Saturday. She couldn't rush off to a job. She had to get rid of him. He was trouble. She closed her eyes and rubbed her forehead where a small headache was beginning. *Why, Lord? How did he find me? Why did he come? Am I safe?*

She lay, ashamed that she hadn't thought to talk to God before about him. She hadn't talked to God about anything since arriving in Wyoming. She'd foolishly believed she was doing just fine on her own—didn't God help those who helped themselves? Or so her grandmother had said.

She heard movement in her small living room. Jack was up. She quickly threw the covers back and dressed in jeans and sweatshirt, limping as quietly as she could around the bedroom. Her ankle was stiff and radiated sharp pain when she used it for support. She didn't want Jack trying to open her door to check on her. She'd shower later. She moved the dresser away from the door with as little noise as possible.

Barefoot, she crossed the hall to the bathroom, placing her crutches softly on the old wood floor, closing the door with only a small squeak and clicking sound. She didn't know why she was sneaking around, it made no sense, but even a minute's delay in facing Jack this morning seemed important. She wanted him gone.

"Morning, Allie," came from the living room. She ignored it as she brushed her hair and then her teeth. She wanted to stay in the bathroom, but felt cowardly and foolish for her desire, knowing it wouldn't solve anything anyway.

She met Jack, standing dressed and smiling, in the small hallway.

"G'morning." She pushed past him with her eyes downcast, wanting to place a crutch on his toes.

"Hey," he grabbed her arm. "Aren't you the grumpy one in the morning?"

"Let me go! I'll get you some breakfast and then we'll talk." She wrenched her arm free and hobbled with her crutches to the kitchen. She experienced a wave of dizziness as she bent down and opened the bottom drawer on the electric range to retrieve a frying pan. She almost dropped the carton of eggs she slid from the fridge, clumsy with fear. She heard Jack close the bathroom door and then a faucet noise. She placed her already cold hands on the cool countertop and forced deep breaths in and out her mouth. *Get a grip. Don't let him see how upset you are.*

She had no idea what all Jack was into, but the conversation she'd overheard in the bathroom at the restaurant that night, and what Phillip had told her, made her insides quake. She knew a little about mobs and the underworld from listening to her father talk and reading the newspapers, and research had shown Jack was involved somehow. Especially when the private investigator informed her who some of Jack's acquaintances were and that his name had been linked, with no proof, to some insider trading of stocks and bonds with some well-known companies. So why did he need her? And what should she do now?

When Jack came back into the kitchen, she forced a smile and said, "Have a seat. I'll have your eggs and bacon ready in a minute, then we can talk." She hoped the way her voice faltered with the last word wasn't noticeable as she turned back to the stove.

CHAPTER SEVEN

"Why do you want to know?" Patrick asked Mac in response to his question about the new teacher.

Examining his fingernails as if checking for dirt, he kept his voice casual. "Well, I need to know how the teacher and you are getting on, don't I?"

"Yeah, I guess so," Patrick replied sitting up in bed. "She's okay. She's pretty and some of the boys are making comments about her at recess. They like her long, blonde hair, even though she wears a ponytail at school."

Mac glanced sharply at Patrick, "Comments? What kind of comments? Are they bad ones?"

"Not really, Dad. Just...you know, comments. Like 'she's hot,' and wondering if she's married and stuff. Hey, I'm missing my cartoons!"

Mac watched Patrick as he raced from the bedroom in his pajamas. Letting him watch TV on Saturday mornings without dressing and brushing his teeth was his weekend treat. Normally, he felt satisfaction in letting his small son have that freedom. Today he sighed in frustration. He'd wanted to pump Patrick some more about Allison. With a sigh, he went back into the kitchen to eat his oatmeal.

It was almost noon when Mac drove his pickup into Sage Flats on the pretext of gassing up for the next veterinary call. The tank was only half empty so he could have waited, but he'd convinced himself he'd better be safe in case he got called to a distant outlying ranch in the middle of the night. However, he found himself driving all the way through the little town, bypassing both gas stations in order to drive by Allison's.

He had the excuse he could pick her up, if she thought she could use her ankle a bit, to go get her car out of the Community Center's parking lot.

No activity was evident around her house, but a black Porsche was parked in her driveway this morning. Jack's maybe? Had he been there all night? *Why didn't I notice the fancy car when I took Allison home last night?*

He slowed as he passed by and wondered if he should stop. He'd not felt this burning need to get tangled in someone else's personal life for a long time. Maybe it was foolishness. Yeah, and maybe it was a nudge he shouldn't ignore. He made a U-turn at the end of the street and headed back to her driveway.

He knocked quietly at first, then harder when he heard voices inside, but no one answered the door. His stomach tightened unreasonably.

Then Allison jerked the door open, her expression hard and unforgiving as she raised her eyes to look into his. A slight relaxing of her mouth made him think she might be relieved to see him.

"I came by to see if we could get your car...uh, maybe Jack could go with me to drive it back if he's here."

She stepped aside so he could enter, and he noted the cozy scene of two places set at the table with sandwiches on the plates. He suddenly felt too big for the small house, and unwelcome, but couldn't think fast enough how to back out of the setting.

"Come in." Allison's voice sounded defeated and tired. Her face was pale with dark circles under her eyes. No sparkle in her eyes today.

"Ah...I could come back later," he stepped in cautiously, ready to turn and run.

"No, you're welcome now. Would you like some lunch? Coffee? Jack and I were just about to start." She pulled out another chair from the table. "Let me take your hat."

He surrendered it, feeling vulnerable without it, but sat down and said, "Just coffee. I already ate at home after I took a short snooze. I was out on a call all night."

"You got called? After you left last night? Did you get any sleep?" She seemed eager to focus on him while Jack patiently chewed and watched them.

"I got a couple hours of sleep after breakfast, but I thought you might be anxious to get your car home, and I needed gas in my pickup, so I came into town." He glanced at Jack, hoping to make him feel included. The guy couldn't be as bad as he seemed last night, could he?

"Drink your coffee and we'll go get her car," Jack spoke up. "Where'd she leave it?"

"In the Community Center parking lot, not far from here."

Mac's hands felt too big for the dainty china cups Allison had sitting in the equally fragile-looking saucers. But that's where his coffee was located, so he squeezed his thumb and forefinger together to lift the cup and prayed he wouldn't spill it. He noticed Jack's long, skinny fingers deftly managed the dainty cups. *Big-city dishes for big-city people,* he thought.

It only took a couple of his western swallows to drain the small cup and say, "Thanks for the coffee. When you're done, Jack, we can be on our way."

It puzzled him that a glance from Allison telegraphed panic if he read it right, but Jack calmly cleaned his plate, put his fork down, and rose from the table.

"Keys, Allie?"

She headed to her bedroom to retrieve them from her purse.

"You're the man!" He slapped Mac on the back as he grabbed the keys from Allison's hand and headed for the door.

Wondering what that meant, Mac followed him, but glanced back at Allison. She stood, balancing on one foot while maintaining a white-knuckled grip on the back of the kitchen chair. He didn't understand the tension that zinged between her and Jack.

Allison watched the men leave, noticing the difference between the two while her mind strung questions together about her options. Jack made her nervous. Mac made her feel safe. How was she going to get rid of Jack?

What does he want from me and why does he need me?

He had stuck to his story all morning that he was in love with her, and that they were meant to be together. *Is he in trouble, and will he bring trouble to me? To Sage Flats?*

She reached for her crutches. She'd clean up the table while she worried. A plate slipped from her hand while trying to hold it as well as a crutch. The resounding crash caused her to jump and lose her balance. A chair caught her as she tipped, and a resounding thump jarred her head as she sat hard on the wooden seat. Caged tears sprang loose, and shattering sobs caused her to bury her head on the table, bumping and spilling her half-drank coffee, which soaked one ear and the side of her head. For a moment she cried harder at the added insult of her clumsiness. And then she stopped.

From somewhere inside her head a voice was speaking, growing stronger as it proclaimed: *What are you doing? You are stronger than this! You are a western woman now, a pioneer of sorts. Think, Allison. You've got to help yourself. There is no one else.*

But another thought crowded in too. Her mother's words to always pray. She hadn't been doing that. She wondered if it would help.

Blotting her hair with a napkin, she rose and again started clearing the table. She could put a little pressure on her foot if she ignored the pain, and used one crutch only, leaving a hand free to carry dishes. Thankfully the kitchen was small, and she managed to transfer everything to the cupboard and stack dirty items by the sink. She grabbed her broom and dustpan and clumsily swept the pieces of the broken ceramic plate into a pile beside a chair. Sitting down again and leaning over she was able to sweep the pieces into the dustpan and then rise and hobble to the waste bin. Exhausted by then, she grabbed the other crutch and swung-thudded her way into the living room, dropping to the couch.

Hot tears scorched a fat trail down her cheeks as her head dropped and she sobbed out her plea, *God, I'm sorry I haven't talked to you. I forgot. What am I going to do? Please make Jack go away again. Please don't let him make trouble, for me, for Mac, or anyone here. Help me know what to do! Lord. Please forgive me for only talking to you now when I'm in trouble. I'll do better, only please help me.*

The sobbing stopped as she sat with eyes squeezed shut and went over her words. Saying them out loud made her feel less alone. It also made her realize how alarmed and desperate she felt. She heard a car door slam and hastily wiped the tears away.

She straightened, forcing courage into her voice as Jack walked in. "You have to leave. I don't want you here. And it looks bad. I'm staying in Sage Flats. Please, just pack up and go."

She could have mistaken the look of hatred and rage on Jack's face at that moment, it was so fleeting, but it made her gasp. Yet she decided she must have imagined it as he suddenly smiled, and the charming, soft voice of a reasonable man came at her from eye level as he squatted in front of her.

"Allie, how can you mean that when we are engaged? I came all the way from New York, halfway across the world to find you!" He swung his arm in a half circle to illustrate the distance he'd been willing to travel to get her back. Expensive deodorant came in a wave of scent that reminded her of New York, and the night in the restaurant. Sudden nausea had her taking a deep breath.

"And I traveled halfway across the world to get away from you! Please, just go, Jack, and I'll forget you were here. If you're in trouble, I won't say anything. Please just go." She hated the fluctuation in her voice.

"Okay, Allie, I'll go, but not far for now. I'm not in trouble. You just need more time. It's okay. I'll be around, I'll stay somewhere close, and we'll see each other. I'll woo you again! I know you still love me. And you're the love of my life, Allie. We belong together. I'm a reasonable man. I can play your game. Just don't make me wait too long, Allie. I might lose patience and then you'll lose me. You don't want that to happen. I'll see you later, Sweetheart. I'll drop by and we'll talk again. Miss me!"

He leaned forward to give her a peck on the forehead then rose and walked over to his duffel bag. Slinging it over his shoulder he saluted her as he exited. She sat stiff and silent until she heard his car door slam and the Porsche start from the back of the house where he'd concealed it the night he came. He had to be hiding from something or someone. A chill ran down her spine.

The breath she hadn't known she was holding swooshed out of her. He'd be back—was that a warning, or a threat?

CHAPTER EIGHT

Mac stopped at the local café for a piece of apple pie and coffee after leaving Jack at Allison's car. He couldn't make himself leave town. He was contemplating driving by her house again when his cell phone rang.

"Got a horse I think has colic," said the voice of one of Mac's long-time customers. "She's laying down and kicking her feet at her stomach. Started about an hour ago. Can you come out?" The man lived fifty miles away. Colic was serious. He had to go.

"Sure," he responded. "See you as soon as I can." Feeling the urgency of getting to a sick animal's side like he always did, he puzzled at a second urgency that made no sense—that he should also hurry to Allison's side. But she had Jack. And he barely knew her. He shrugged, grabbed his hat off the table, drew out enough money from his billfold for pie and a tip, and left.

As Mac drove back to his clinic to pick up more supplies before heading to the rancher's sick horse, a black Porsche with tinted windows swung onto Main Street ahead of him, ignoring a stop sign and squealing its tires as it accelerated and headed out of town. Sticking out like the proverbial sore thumb in this world of pickups and economy cars, even before he checked the license plate, he knew it had to be Jack. Maybe he was finally leaving town. He hoped so, for Allison's sake. Okay, maybe he wanted Jack gone for his sake too. He shrugged as he left the city limits. No business of his. He tried to ignore the little bloom of hope unfolding in his heart.

Allison took deep breaths as she placed a call to her parents.

"Good morning. White residence," a practiced female voice answered. Some of Allison's tension seeped out at the sound of Cecile's familiar voice. Cecile was her parents' live-in housekeeper and cook. Right now, she represented normalcy.

"Is Mom or Dad there?" Allison asked her.

"Your mom is napping, and your dad's at the office even though it's Saturday, but you know him. Should I wake your mom for you?"

"No," Allison quickly assured her. "I'll call Dad at the office. Tell Mom I only called to chat and will catch her again. Everything's fine here. Nice talking to you, Cecile!" She ended the call and hastily connected to her father's backline work number. He answered on the second ring.

"Dad?" Her voice wobbled. She made an effort to steady it. "Did you know Jack is here?" She meant to ease into it, but fear had her blurting it out.

"Jack? Jack Corbel? How'd he find you?" A big breath of relief rushed out of her. At least her father hadn't divulged her whereabouts.

"That's what I was wondering. He's tracked me somehow. He's ruining everything, Dad." She hated the near sob that followed her words. "I don't want him here. I don't understand what he wants from me, but I don't want him anymore. He's into something I think, Dad, back in New York. It's maybe mob-related. I had Phillip check up on him and he told me Jack has friends in the mob."

"Are you sure? Why did you ask Phillip to check up on him?"

"I'd overheard something in the restaurant one night, in the bathroom, before two couples Jack and I were dining with showed up. Two women I didn't know, but later met as our dinner partners, were discussing someone named Jack. They said he might be interested in a woman he was with because her dad would be a lawyer and could keep him out of jail.

"I had no idea what, or even who, they were talking about until I got back to the table and saw they were Jack's friends.

"That's why I broke the engagement, not because I didn't love him. I started feeling scared around him and his friends. I told you I didn't love him because I didn't want to tell you the real reason, but I guess I should have. I didn't want you to worry, and I thought I'd be done with him when I left.

"Mom didn't tell him where I am, did she? I know you both thought a lot of him."

Her flow of words finally stopped. It felt good to say things she'd previously kept from her parents, but it also accentuated her fear and confusion about why Jack wanted her.

"No, your mom hasn't had any contact with him. Honey, are you all right? Is he with you now? Is he staying with you?"

"No, I mean, he stayed on my couch last night. I told him he had to leave this morning. But says he's coming back. He brought the engagement ring with him. I don't think he'll leave. He's scaring me a little."

"Do you want me to come out there?"

Her dad would if she wanted him to, but it would take him a couple of days to make arrangements. He'd have to fly to Casper, then rent a car to drive the 100 miles to Sage Flats. She wanted answers faster than that. A lot could happen in three or four days. Jack seemed determined to take her back to New York with him. "Can you check on what's happening with him back in New York? He says he 'needs' me and I wonder why. I think he's into something shady, Dad. Can you check as soon as possible? Even before Monday?"

"I'll try," her father reassured. But she could hear the questions in his voice. Being an only child, she'd never had to vie for his affections with siblings, however, his love for and time spent on his chosen career as an attorney sometimes left her feeling neglected. But she knew she came first if she was ever in trouble. She just wasn't sure if she *was* in trouble or not.

"Thanks, Dad. Let me know as soon as you can. Call me on my cell phone." She didn't want Jack picking up her Sage Flats home phone if he came back and figured out she might be calling for help. She was so glad the old home still had a landline in place, and she could give that number to whomever she pleased. The landlords, an older couple who'd moved out of state to be closer to their children, included the bill for it in her monthly rent, keeping ownership in their name. She wasn't sure she liked them knowing about any long-distance calls she took part in, but hadn't really planned to use it for long-distance when she moved in. They seemed so trusting, and she liked having another option in case something happened to her cell.

Feeling unsettled, but unable to pace to wear off her nervous energy due to her injury, she called Penny. "I've got my car back!"

"How's your ankle? And what about the care our local vet gave you?"

"You knew I thought he was a real doctor, *didn't* you? You rascal! My ankle is still pretty sore. I'm afraid to try driving. Can't get around without my crutches. Don't know how I'll make it to school Monday!"

"Well," Penny paused, "I suppose I can come pick you up, unless you can get that fake doctor to pick you up!"

"You know I didn't mean he was a fake, he's just not a people doctor. But I got over it; he's really quite nice."

"Ya, and you better hang on to him if he's interested. He hasn't shown any interest in any of the other single gals that have crossed his path. And not because they haven't tried to catch his attention. He's pretty much all business around everyone. My guess is he hasn't gotten over his wife. She died a couple of years ago. Gotta go, but keep me posted if you want a ride Monday. See ya, Girlfriend."

Allison couldn't bring herself to say anything about Jack to Penny. Fear, shame, and vulnerability caused her silence, she supposed.

Finally, it was "suppertime"—in ranch lingo—she'd learned that when she'd missed a lunch with Penny, thinking "dinner" meant an evening meal. Breakfast, dinner, and supper were the order in Sage Flats territory. Lunch was in between and meant a snack.

She wasn't hungry so grabbed a stack of fifth-grade papers to grade. Her ears continued to listen for the return of Jack.

Her hand jerked at the loud knocking on her door, causing a dark nasty-looking check mark to mar a young girl's paper.

CHAPTER NINE

For a moment, she stared at the door, frozen. The knock came again. Not like Jack's knock, she realized. The nerve endings calmed a little as she prayed it wasn't him. She glanced out her kitchen window. With the sun already behind the red buttes to the west, dusk seemed like an entity pressing against her house. Dark silhouettes of trees guarded her house, or maybe hemmed her in.

"Who's there?" Her hand cradled the doorknob.

"Mac," the deep voice said.

Tension released in a whispered "Thank you, God" as she opened the door and stepped back.

Mac ducked and removed his good-guy hat as he came in. His presence chased away the fears in her heart.

"Just thought I'd stop and say 'howdy,' on my way home from a sick call."

"A sick call?" She hadn't seen him, nor Jack, all day. The relief at which man was standing in front of her made her want to fall into his arms.

"I had a horse with colic, on a ranch about fifty miles out. Long day." He rubbed his face and, pushing an errant shock of strawberry-blond hair into place, resettled his hat on his head.

"You hungry? Have you eaten?" She fidgeted with her hands. They wanted to touch that lock of hair.

His eyes searched her face. "Yes, and no."

"Would you like some eggs? A sandwich? I could fix you something." She needed him to stay. Jack and darkness were double dangers waiting to pounce. *Why do I feel safe with a relative stranger, and frightened of a former fiancé?*

"Let's go to the café. They have a great hot hamburger with real mashed potatoes. I need comfort food. How about you? How's your ankle?"

"My ankle's just a little sore, painful only if I step wrong. I have it wrapped. Are you sure? We can eat here." *Where was Jack? Would he be back tonight?* She had a sudden urge to gather her pajamas, makeup, and toothbrush and ask to go home with Mac.

"Let's go to the restaurant! Wear a coat. Evening chill is moving in. I'm suddenly hungrier than I thought!"

When she was ready to leave, he crooked an elbow her way and she grabbed it—security was a denim work jacket with a strong arm inside. She could forego the crutches if she was careful.

A light scent of soap and fresh air wafted from him and teased her senses. A refreshing, honest smell. *He must have taken the trouble to go home and clean up before coming over. I won't question why he's here, Lord. I'm just grateful he is.*

He walked slowly, accommodating her halting gate. It felt right. She mentally reminded herself she wasn't able to recognize "right" in a man.

The café was warm and noisy with a few ranch families eating while their kids traded tables to be with friends, or squirted ketchup on hamburgers and fingers, all probably returning from Saturday shopping in Casper. Allison tried to imagine what their homes might be like—log perhaps, braided rugs in the entry, soft lights highlighting leather sofas—scenes from a magazine she'd thumbed through once producing a foreign longing in her heart.

"What can I get you?" The waitress stood with a small pad and pencil ready for their order and looked at Allison.

Allison jerked her dreaming mind back to the task of answering the shapely young female in her sparkling white uniform. She saw speculation, maybe even animosity in the hazel eyes framed by dyed-red, frizzy hair, as they glared down at her. A glance at the good doc, who smiled engagingly at the woman even though he was ignored, had her wondering if there was history between the two. Why should she care?

"Hot hamburger, double the potatoes," Mac inserted. "And a chocolate malt, a cup of coffee, and another piece of that apple pie if you have any left." The waitress wrote it down, her eyes on the notepad, still ignoring her smiling customer.

"I'd like a cup of soup if you have any?" Allison ventured, wondering at the woman's unfriendly and closed expression. "And could I have a glass of milk?" She closed her eyes. She sounded like a small child. What had happened to the secure teacher of fifth graders?

"Got some homemade bean! That do?"

"Yes, thank you," she tried for more volume, "and if you have a..." her voice disappeared as Jack entered the café door.

"And?" the waitress leaned toward her as if coaxing a reluctant toddler to finish a sentence.

"Nothing more, that's all." Allison's chest tightened, and she found it hard to suck in enough air as the unfriendly woman left.

"There's your fiancé." Mac's voice had acquired an edge and his smile was gone.

"I told you, he's not my fiancé anymore." Her shoulders sagged as her hands fell to her lap. She watched Jack grab the shoulder of their waitress as she headed toward the kitchen with their order. The woman's lips, compressed in irritation, relaxed and turned into smiling lips as he enthralled her with something he said. Allison grimaced as she remembered the many times she had been annoyed at him, and he had charmed her into submission to accomplish whatever he wanted. He dripped with charisma when he chose.

"Hey, Allie, this is where you are! I went by the house to invite you to dinner, but I see you already found someone to buy it for you. How clever...you haven't been in town all that long and you've picked up a faithful friend to take care of you! Lonesome feelings will get you in trouble you know. Good thing I'm here now." His tone of voice lowered intimately as he slid into the booth beside her.

He jerked a head nod. "Mac. Thanks for bringing Allie for a meal. She can always use the nourishment. Are you staying to join us? I'll take my fiancée home when we're done eating. I appreciate your looking after her for me."

Allison looked at the man across the table to find his Adam's apple bobbing, one cheek muscle twitching, and his ears turning red. A flitting thought of how animated he looked was extinguished by the realization of how angry he must be.

"Jack," she placed her hand on his arm, a mistake she recognized when he covered it with his own hand. "Jack, Mac brought me and will take me home. You don't have to bother. Did you get a room somewhere?" She had to know if he planned on staying with her tonight.

"Yeah, but I'll take you back to that old house you're staying in. I got a room at that dinky, rundown motel near the highway. Man, they don't offer much in the Wild West, do they? The sink is stained with brown water, the bed's hard, and there's only a couple of plug-ins. Impossible to use the computer, alarm, and TV at the same time! How'd you find this podunk place anyway, Sweetheart? You must have been really broken up after you lost me."

Mac's teeth were making a gritting sound now. She almost expected steam to come out his ears and his stare at Jack to burn holes in her former fiancé's face.

"It's not a podunk place; I was not broken up, and I like it. Why don't you go back to New York and whatever sleazy deal you're involved in now?" She'd found her ability to speak her mind, show her temper, and abandon all caution, in one sentence.

Jack's face changed from affable to calculating as it moved closer to hers. His words squeezed out through compressed lips.

"I am not involved in something sleazy! Where did you find that word, Sweetheart?" A practiced orator, the vexed tone of his voice became honeyed and gentle. "How could you accuse the one person you love of something sleazy? All my business deals are above reproach, and they buy you nice things. Remember the diamond? I'm keeping it for you. Remember the nightclubs? The terrific friends I've introduced you to? Not cowpunchers and sheep herders, Allie. Real people who are successful. Not backwoodsmen like you'll run into out here. Come to your senses and come back to New York with me. We'll leave in the morning. Eat your soup." The meal had come.

Allison saw Mac staring at his mega-mound of mashed potatoes and gravy as if he was ready to scoop it up and stuff it down Jack's throat. Her stomach shrank, leaving no room for food as Jack began to cut the rare T-bone steak he'd ordered.

Fear Mac would walk out, and fear he wouldn't, pressed against her heart. *What do I do?* she begged God silently. *Help me out of this.*

The song "Home on the Range" played from inside her purse.

"Let me out," she pushed at Jack's side. "I need to answer my phone," she couldn't keep the urgency out of her voice.

Jack stopped eating and looked at her. "Answer it, Darling. I'm sure Mac won't mind, and we have no secrets, do we?" She knew guilt shone in her eyes and closed them. She hated her helplessness.

"No, I suppose not. Probably spam anyway." She put the cell away as it quit ringing, relieved at not having to talk in front of her ex-fiancé and disappointed at not being able to take the call. She was certain it was her father.

She dipped a spoon in her now lukewarm soup, blowing on it unnecessarily, trying for normalcy in the midst of the tension-filled booth.

"Eat, Jack, and let's go back to my house," she said, acceding to his demand that he take her home. She knew no other way to avoid a confrontation.

She sent an apologetic look Mac's way. "I guess Jack will take me back. I appreciate you bringing me to the restaurant, Mac." She tilted her head and smiled at him, trying to convey her regret, her insecurity, and her wish to prevent conflict between the two men.

Mac got up, put his hat on, and left the full plate of food. He hadn't uttered a word, but Allison got the drift of his thoughts only too well. He was disgusted with her and the smooth-talking man beside her.

She wouldn't be seeing him around again. Just as well. Her entanglement with the man at her side was too complicated, too risky, and maybe too dangerous. She would never want Mac to keep her safe if it meant harm to himself. What was she going to do?

CHAPTER TEN

Mac walked back to the truck, setting his hat on his head with a firmer hand than needed, boots stomping and raising tiny puffs of dust in the gravel parking lot. He hadn't experienced this much frustration since his marriage. Realization slowed his steps and sent his mind in a different direction. To Catherine. The familiar feelings of sorry and regret settled in, and alongside them a new feeling he couldn't name yet. But his heart was involved somehow.

Mac cautioned himself, remembering his friend, Cody. Cody had taken a load of cattle to market the previous fall to Cheyenne and met a female auctioneer. Her unusual choice of career, plus her outgoing personality and pretty face, easily hooked the young rancher. He'd spent two months traveling weekly from his ranch to Cheyenne, a 140-mile trip one-way, only to find out she had two other suckers on the hook too, and true to her profession, would go to the highest bidder. Cody, who'd never been married, had sworn off women. It was the second time he'd been burned.

While Mac hadn't had that kind of luck before, he thought it might be his turn now. That sweet-looking schoolteacher appeared to have a wagonload of trouble, and she'd drag that load right into a relationship. So, why did he even wonder what was in that wagon? And want to help her unload it?

He went home, kissed his sleeping son lightly on the forehead, and entered his own bedroom, sitting down heavily on his bed. He stared at the wedding picture showing him and Catherine gazing into each other's eyes. A longing so intense passed through him, tears gathered in his throat. He swallowed them down. Crying came easy to him and ended with a headache most times.

Two years gone by since her death. Such a short time, yet a lifetime ago. Was he being disloyal? They shared a child, a living part of each of them.

Rationally, he figured he needed to find someone else. Catherine would be okay with that. Life was about relationships, with God and fellow humans. Maybe he was ready to try love again. But guilt still wedged its way between his thoughts.

Help me, Lord. What is this thing with Allison about? Helping a fellow human being, or something personal? Am I supposed to be this confused?

No answer came. He sat staring at the 5 X 7 photo until his eyes blurred with tiredness.

By the time he'd undressed and turned out the light, a peace moved through him. He relaxed into the knowing that since he'd asked, God would work it out for him. There would be bumps on the road to the answers, that's how life worked, but he'd continue the prayers for help, knowing they were heard by someone with more wisdom than he had.

He angled his head toward the picture, barely visible now in the moonlight. Catherine was still his best friend, living in his heart. It was okay to move on. If Allison was part of that process, it would make itself clear in time. He hoped.

He checked that his phone was on and at his bedside and closed his eyes on a prayer of praise.

"Done?" Jack grabbed the bill from the table shortly after Mac left. Allison dabbed her mouth with the paper napkin; the soup might reappear any minute. She took deep breaths while he laid cash down.

"Yes, let's go." She was relieved. And worried. Jack would come back to her house now. *Would he stay or go to his motel? Would he expect something other than a quick "Good night"?*

She wanted to check her cell phone. Did her dad leave a message? What had he said?

Jack escorted her to the car with a hand on her elbow. It felt like a restraint. The ride to her house was silent. When they arrived, he followed her in.

"We need to discuss your coming back, Allie."

"I'm not coming back! I have a job here. I'm teaching fifth grade." She wished her voice had more conviction. She laid her purse on the kitchen table.

"Allie..." He drew it out like he was reasoning with a child. "You know you're just rebelling. I maybe pushed you in New York, was too fast in assuming you were ready to get married. But I can't live without you. I came all this way to take you back. We can get married, take a long honeymoon, go to Mexico or Europe! I love you.

"Remember our plans? I'll even take on your name. I see your independence is important. We can be Allison and Jack White! Come on, Allie. Let's go back tomorrow. We'll take a little side trip on the way, see more of the west if you want. You don't have to stay in this hick town. You're destined for better. We can even go to Vegas and get married right away!"

His voice had an urgency she didn't understand. His hands were palm up, stretched out to her. He seemed...afraid. This was not Jack.

She opened her mouth to say...what? He'd thrown her. Things were out of kilter. *What was wrong with him?*

"I...I can't." Her words caught in her throat. The atmosphere changed; tension sang between them.

"Fine!" he shouted, grabbing a chair and throwing it across the room. "Sit in this hole and rot! Your last chance at being somebody. And you blew it! I'm gone!" He wrenched the door open and slammed it shut behind him. She heard a loud crack from somewhere on the old dry frame.

Allison stood, frozen in place, as were her emotions. What had happened? She'd never seen Jack so edgy, displaying his temper.

Smooth and suave—that was Jack. She righted the chair and sank onto it, staring at the wall. What now?

"Lock the door," a small voice said in the back of her mind. She obeyed, limping the short distance to it, her agitation making her hands almost too weak to turn the deadbolt. The squeal of tires and roar of an engine signified he was gone. *Is he gone for good? Or will he be back?*

Her cell phone beeped. She pulled it out of her purse and saw a text from her dad. When she opened the app, her breathing stopped as she read the short message: *A "person of interest" is being sought in the mysterious disappearance of a member of one of the "families" here. Call me right away.*

Her unsteady hands almost dropped the small phone. She punched the button that would dial her dad directly. There was a two-hour time difference between Wyoming and New York. She hoped her dad was still awake.

"Allison?" Her dad's voice was strong and demanding in her ear.

"Yes. What do you mean, Dad? What does that information you texted have to do with me?"

CHAPTER ELEVEN

Sunday morning sun warmed Mac's face, and fingers of light poked their way between his lids. He opened, then quickly closed his eyes against the rude intrusion. He should have pulled the shade before he fell asleep, but he'd been staring at the moon, thinking of Allison and Catherine when his brain had finally shut down.

A puzzle. Allison was an enchanting puzzle, kind of like the leprechauns he'd heard about as a young boy. Was she bent on mischief, collecting men like the leprechauns collected gold coins? Or was she a beautiful maiden, pursued by an evil villain, and he, Mac, was meant to rescue her, like in an old-time melodrama?

Mac shook his head at his whimsical thoughts and threw the covers back, charging out of bed with sudden energy. He would invite her to church.

"Paddy!" He knelt beside his son's bed and reached to tousle the spiky red hair pointing several different directions as it peeked out above the blankets.

"Dad! Quit it!" A youthful arm flopped out of the sheets in a random arc, seeking Mac's hand to bat it away.

"C'mon, Squirt, rise and shine. Time to get ready for Sunday School. Let's see if Miss White can go with us, should we?" He hadn't meant to say that, to put his sudden desire into words. She and the city slicker were probably laughing together over the cow town vet suckered into taking her out for supper. Suddenly his mood soured like last week's milk. How dumb could he be?

Patrick's head popped up like a ground squirrel's looking for danger.

"You mean it, Dad? We can ask her? That'd make Greg jealous. He's got a crush on her." Greg was Paddy's best friend in school. The young son's eyes were wide open now and searching Mac's face.

"Well, I suppose we could check it out. She might not want to," Mac answered, backpedaling, wondering if he was presumptuous. Why would she even entertain the thought of going anywhere with them when Jack was probably with her?

"Call her!" Boyish enthusiasm was beautiful to behold, despite the fact it was only eight in the morning.

"Let's wait awhile, maybe she's not up yet." Courage was sliding back down into the hole from which it had sprung so hopefully.

"What's her phone number? I'll call her." His now totally awake offspring bounced out of bed and ran toward the kitchen wall phone.

That's when Mac realized he didn't even *have* her number. How stupid.

"I don't have it."

"What? You don't have it? Da...ad," he drew the name out, noticeably disgusted with his dense parent. "Why didn't you get her number?" The voice turned whiney.

"It never occurred to me I'd want it," he lied. "Well, maybe we'll just drive by her house and see if she's up. Get dressed, Sport, let's have breakfast. We'll leave a little early." Mac headed to the kitchen to set out cereal bowls as Patrick raced to his closet and snatched a shirt off a hanger causing the hanger to snap and fly across the room.

"Slow down!" Mac yelled, then directed the words to himself. He barely knew Allison. Why couldn't he clear her from his mind? What was the urgency leaving him breathless and his hands fumbling the silverware this morning?

Mrs. Thompson came out of her bedroom in her blue flannel robe as they were heading out the door an hour later. "Off to church? Have a nice morning." She waved them off.

Sunday was her day to sleep in if Mac was home, and he got Paddy up so they could go to worship service and Sunday school. If he wasn't home, Paddy didn't go. Mrs. Thompson was a top-notch housekeeper, cook, and babysitter, but to Mac's regret, didn't attend any church.

"We'll eat dinner in town," he called to her as she retreated down the hall. He'd grown up with those country terms, lost them while attending Veterinary College, and was happy to apply them to his day again—breakfast, dinner, supper. Lunch was pie and coffee. He'd noticed Allison was getting the hang of them too.

After they were buckled in, he backed his truck out of the garage and turned toward town, cruising through the empty streets to Allison's little rental on the east side. His sweaty hands gripped the steering wheel. Carefully, he wiped each hand on his new, stiff jeans, trusting they wouldn't turn blue from the dye. He prayed his new "Super-dry, Clean Scent" antiperspirant worked.

Patrick was chattering, and Mac didn't have a clue what it was about. He felt like a teenager again, excited and unsure.

No cars except Allison's in the yard. Good. Dare he stop? Sure, just a friend saying good morning.

A frisson of apprehension skated up his spine. It seemed too quiet and lifeless around the place.

"Wait here." His instruction came out stilted, terse. Patrick stopped talking and gave him a curious glance.

"What's wrong, Dad?"

"Nothing, I hope. Just wait here." He turned off the ignition and left the vehicle, scanning the area as he walked to the door and knocked. No one responded. He rapped his knuckles against the wood again, glancing down to notice a fracture in the wood frame. The crack hadn't weathered yet. When and how had that happened?

When his knocking elicited no response, he walked around the house to inspect the back where he knew an old porch existed, denoting what used to be the front. Now overgrown weeds strove to hide the old gravel street that passed by. The town had shrunk, and only a couple of sagging shacks with peeling paint stood forlorn and abandoned beyond Allison's home.

The old front door was swollen shut. It obviously hadn't been opened recently. He noticed what looked like a good-sized pile of fresh sod partially hidden by long grass and wild sunflowers about a hundred feet from the house. He'd have to warn Allison about skunks and badgers digging in the dirt. Hopefully, she wasn't scared of the small, native animals that sometimes wandered through yards on the edge of town. Something about the size of that dirt pile didn't seem right though. Maybe he'd examine it closer someday. It looked like the grass was pressed down in places too, probably some animal wandering through, and he dismissed it from his mind as he wondered where Allison was.

He walked back around to the door now used as the front entrance and knocked again. As he was about to give up, wondering if she'd gone somewhere with Jack, the door slowly opened.

This was a different Allison than the one he had met at the dance. She looked vulnerable in the droop of her head, uncombed hair, and sleep-glazed eyes. A fluffy pink bathrobe was tightly cinched around her slender body. She clutched the frame and listed to one side, keeping her right foot off the floor. Immediate concern had his arm reaching for her elbow and inserting himself partway through the opening.

"What's wrong? Are you hurt? Are you okay? Is your ankle worse?"

Her eyes widened and locked on his.

"Yes! Yes, no, I'm fine, I...overslept I guess." She turned from him and looked about the kitchen as if seeking an excuse for her behavior, or his.

"May I come in? Are you alone?" He couldn't lose the feeling something was wrong.

"Oh, I'm sorry. Of course, come in." She backed up a couple of limping steps, still gripping the knob with whitened knuckles and giving a small gasp as she put pressure on her injury.

Mac glanced back at the pickup to make sure his inquisitive son was still inside. He waved at the boy's expectant expression and moved into the kitchen, closing the door.

"What's wrong, Allison? Has something happened? Where's Jack?" He had momentarily forgotten why he'd stopped in, his gut tightening with each question.

"Jack?" She stared past him at the wall. "He...he left. Last night. Angry."

"Angry? Why?"

"I don't know for sure. I've never seen him act that way. I refused to go with him again, and he got really mad and left. He threw a chair across the room. It's okay. He's gone. That's all that matters."

Her wrinkled forehead and downward gaze said it wasn't all that mattered.

"Threw a chair across the room? Did he hurt you? Is something else wrong?" He gently cradled her shoulders with his hands. "Tell me!"

Allison burst into tears. A second later, Mac's arms folded around her, and his white cotton shirt muffled her sobs.

The kitchen door slammed back against the wall.

"Dad! I'm tired of waiting! What's taking so..." His mouth gaped open. "You're hugging Ms. White?"

"Uh, no. Yes. I'm just comforting her, like I do you when you're upset," he improvised.

Allison left the shelter of Mac's embrace and reached for a napkin from the nearby table to wipe her eyes and blow her nose.

"I'm fine." She turned watery eyes toward Paddy. "I felt sad for a minute and your dad gave me a hug to make me feel better! And I do! See?" She flashed him a big tremulous smile. "What were you waiting for?" She flicked a look at Mac before returning her gaze to the small boy so full of enthusiasm that he seemed to be dancing in place.

"Dad was supposed to ask you to go to church with us. Didn't he ask you yet?" Paddy frowned in disgust at his parent's obvious slowness.

Mac cleared his throat, not quite recovered from the quick change of scene. "I was getting around to it," he said, his eyes on Allison. "Do you think you could handle going with us this morning?"

"I...I don't know. I haven't gotten dressed. I'd make you late. You two better go on. I'll go some other time." She kept her eyes downward, focused on hands squeezing each other together repeatedly as she spoke.

"Please!" her young student pleaded. "Come with us. We can wait, can't we, Dad?" He turned puppy eyes to his father.

Sensing something was still terribly wrong and experiencing a fear of leaving her home alone, Mac took up the cause. "Yes, it's okay if we're a little late. I'd have called, but I didn't know your phone number. I'll make you some coffee while you change. We'll eat at the café after church. Is this your coffee maker?" He moved to the small counter space where the appliance sat as if the matter was decided.

"I...I don't think I should go. I'm a mess and I can't get ready in time. Just you two go." Now *she* had puppy eyes.

"No!" He was too loud. He gentled. "No, we'll wait. Please, come with us."

Her arm lifted then dropped. She turned toward her bedroom.

Mac sighed. What could be so wrong with Jack? And, as he pondered that, he wondered why that pile of soil in her backyard bothered him.

CHAPTER TWELVE

Allison stripped off her robe and nightgown and sorted through outfits in her closet. She couldn't concentrate and passed by outfits that would have been perfect if she hadn't been seeing the last scene with Jack and replaying the phone call with her father in her head.

"An important mob family member disappeared three days ago here," her father had said. "That person was married to a don's daughter. Some think he may have been murdered. It seems your former fiancé might be another family member who is missing. Like you said, I found he has ties to these people. Phillip told me when he heard about the situation." Apprehension had begun to sing along her nerve endings.

"Yes, Phillip said Jack had mobster friends. I don't know much about the structure within the mob though. What's a don?" She held her breath, wondering if she was in some kind of bad dream.

"A don is a leader in the Mafia—an important leader. Phillip found out Jack is a person of interest, to the police and to the mob, maybe to more than one mob family," he'd continued. "And he's disappeared also, but you and I know he's been in Sage Flats. I haven't told anyone you've seen him. I don't want you involved in this. Is he still there with you, Honey? Can you get rid of him? Tell him you're not interested? Are you safe?"

Allison, frozen with shock, had gripped the cell phone in her hand until her fingers cramped. Then she'd connected the dots. *Could Jack be a murderer?* His recent display of temper had zipped through her mind. Her gaze had flown to her door, checking that it was locked. She'd swayed with weakness and stumbled to her sofa, scarcely mindful of the lingering pain in her ankle.

"Are you sure, Dad? You're sure you're talking about *my* Jack?"

"Yes. Is he still there?"

She hadn't known how to answer. If she'd said, "Yes," as she'd longed to do, her father would be concerned for her safety and move mountains to come to her. He would have to at least fly over them, she thought a bit hysterically, to be at her side. But Jack had left. She hoped.

"Why do you ask?" she'd queried, stalling for time to consider the things he'd just said.

"Well, if he is, I think he might be dangerous. Is he there?" he'd asked for the third time. His words had been clipped and closer together, a sure sign he was agitated.

"No! You don't have to worry. He's gone, I mean, he's not here. He's not coming back." She continued to pray the latter was the truth. She hated lying to her father.

"I'll let you know if he does. Thanks for warning me. I hope they find him!" She'd had to end the conversation to think. "Call me if you find out anything more! And don't give my address or phone number out to anyone! Please tell Mom too. Okay? I've got to go. Thanks again for checking things out, but so far everything's fine here."

"All right, Honey." He'd paused, and she'd wondered if he believed everything was fine. "Let me know the minute you hear from Jack, if you do."

"Sure, Dad. Don't worry. Love you."

He'd responded in kind, and she'd snapped her phone shut, feeling vulnerable and isolated at the loss of connection. Closing her eyes, she'd forced herself to take deep breaths to lose the tension and fear pooling in her stomach that had birthed nausea.

She needed to install a different lock on her door. Maybe put two deadbolts on. But her former love, who now seemed a stranger, had climbed through a window when he'd arrived. She'd have to get someone to install locks on them too. Then she'd buy a weapon.

Where in this little town would she get a gun? She hadn't fallen asleep until the sun peeked over the horizon and chased the monsters lurking in the shadows away.

Her mind refocusing back to the present, she yanked a green cotton shirtwaist off its hanger and dressed in under a minute. Slipping on sandals, she hobbled across the hall to the bathroom and brushed her hair and teeth, unable to prevent a small gasp each time she stepped wrong on her injured limb.

A cool wet washcloth blanched some of the redness from her eyes and cheeks, foundation did the rest. She grabbed a mascara wand and made a swipe at her lashes, opened her lipstick, dropped it in her haste, and bit back a wayward word. Retrieving it from behind the stool, where dropped things always rolled, she colored her lips and throwing the tube into a drawer, hobbled into the kitchen.

Paddy sat slumped over with chin in hands. His father was washing dishes. A steaming cup of coffee on the table beckoned her.

She clutched it, burning her tongue as she took two quick gulps.

"I'm ready!" She felt excited and giddy, and enormous relief she wasn't going to be home alone. Rehashing the conversation with her dad in her head had upset her all over again.

Mac rinsed the last dish and opened the sink stopper. "Okay, let's go," he said cheerfully, wiping his hands on the kitchen towel and turning toward her. His hands stilled with the towel yet in their grip, and he stared at her. Her heart did a small flip at the look in his eyes and on his face. Caring, admiration, and tenderness seemed transmitted in that look. She knew she must be fantasizing and looked away.

Paddy jumped up and ran for the truck. After they were all out, Allison locked the house and followed, almost groaning when she saw what they were riding to church in—a veterinarian's pickup. She grimaced. What was that brown stuff on the side?

As if knowing her thoughts, Mac apologized. "Sorry about the coach, Milady, but it's the only vehicle I have. A poor country vet can't have too many monthly bills, you ken? I hope you don't mind?"

"Oh, no!" she lied. "I ascertained your fortune, sir, when I found out you weren't a 'people' doctor and didn't usually take your patients to the local emergency room!"

Mac looked at her face, her focus seemed to be on walking with the crutches, but a slight upturn of lips gave away her attempt at jesting. He was amazed at the abrupt change from looking worried and fearful to playful in such a short time. Maybe he'd read her wrong.

"Ah, but a country vet is ever so important." He thickened his brogue. "If no one tended to the cows, from whence would come your Beef Wellington, your Prime Rib, your Porterhouse Steak?" He took her hand, offering support as she attempted the high climb into her seat after Paddy leaped in. She put her sprained ankle in, putting extra weight on Mac's helping hand as she perched on her left leg.

"This isn't going to work," She turned her head, looking at his face just inches from her, and his lungs forgot to exhale.

"I don't think I can do this." She dropped her gaze and returned her injured foot to the ground.

Able to get his breathing going again, Mac asked, "May I?" At her nod, he circled one arm around her shoulders and placed another behind her knees. He lifted her into the cab, amazed his jittery arms were up to the task. He'd carried her to his truck the night she'd fallen with no problem. What had come over him?

His son, thankfully, helped him put his confusion aside as the small boy struggled with the seat belt and commented, "I'm sure glad you're going with us. I'm going to tell my Sunday School class. It's cool!"

"Thanks, Paddy. I'm pleased that you're happy I'm coming with you. It's nice to spend time with you outside of regular school. What are you learning in Sunday School?"

"Oh, the usual. Oh...except we're studying about Samson. Did you know he was really strong? He might have worked out at a gym or something, you know, like a Roman gym? But he was strong because he had long hair. Dad, if I grow my hair long, will I be strong?" The young boy looked hopefully up at his dad.

Mac glanced down at his pride and joy. "Only if God tells you to grow long hair so you will be strong, Buddy."

"Oh," Paddy said, and went back to his story. "He must have been busy fighting the Phillipstings, the Philly...aw, I can't remember the name, but he did a lot of fighting. And then he fell in love with someone pretty. I don't remember her name, but she made him tell her why he was strong and cut off his hair while he was sleeping! Wasn't that mean? She was a bad lady."

He went on to recite more of the Bible story, interpreted Paddy-style, but Allison's thoughts were inadvertently thrust back into her nightmare regarding Jack, with Paddy's mispronunciation of the Philistines bringing Phillip's name and his investigation to mind again. Her heart missed a beat and sharp-edged fear cut into her effort to pay attention to the story being told beside her.

She jerked back to awareness as the vehicle hit a pothole in the parking area of the church. They stopped a few feet beyond the jarring event, and Mac exited, coming around to open her door. Too excited to wait, Paddy slid out Mac's side and raced for the church's entrance.

Mac helped her slide from the seat to the ground, handed her the crutches, then kept his hand on her back as they headed toward a white-framed building with a swinging bell clanging loudly in a tower on top. Her eyes lifted to the sight for a moment, then nervous, and trying to minimize her halting gait, she scanned the other churchgoers to see who watched, thinking Mac's hand on her waist showed a tentative claim on her as his girl. She called herself silly for even having such a thought and decided to relax when only a few people glanced her way. She was so confused about her life and safety right now, she might stumble without the strength in that nearby hand ready to steady her. She tried not to notice how secure it made her feel.

The order and reverence of the service did nothing to calm the uncertainty and sense of danger causing her heart to skip beats, and she found it hard to focus on the songs and sermon. Only when the worship quartet sang the song "I'll Fly Away" did she tune in. Oh, how she wished she could fly away right now.

She seemed to be floating in a state of illusion, with the real world only brushing against her now and then. But she noted the alarm on Mac's face when she lowered her voice and asked him as they walked out of the church, "Where can I buy a gun?"

CHAPTER THIRTEEN

"A gun!" Mac's growly voice was low but penetrating. A couple a few feet ahead of them peeked back but kept on walking. Allison waited until the distance from them lengthened. She looked at Mac's face, squinting her eyes against the sun.

"Yes. Don't you have a gun? Doesn't everyone out here have a gun?" Belatedly realizing her question seemed out of place for a big-city gal, she tried to cover. "I simply thought being single and all, and maybe doing a little sightseeing, I might scare up a snake...I might be better off with something to defend myself with! Do they sell them in Sage Flats?"

"Well, Dave at the hardware store has a few, and can order one in. Have you ever owned one? Ever shot one?"

"No. But don't you just point and pull the trigger? How hard can it be? Don't other women here carry them?"

"Some," he acknowledged. They stood by his truck waiting for Paddy to finish talking to his friend Greg. Mac's wrinkled brow and squinted eyes didn't lessen the clear sky-blue of his irises as he looked at her. Of course, he'd be curious about her request. She decided she better play it down now that she was aware of a place to inquire about purchasing self-protection.

"Oh, well, if you think I don't need one, I probably shouldn't get one."

"No, if you want one, I can teach you how to shoot. I can help you look for one too, take you to Dave's Hardware next Saturday, and talk to Dave with you. He might have some to try out." His voice took on an eager note.

"Well, I'll see...let you know. That might be nice." She needed one as soon as possible. She had no intention of waiting until Saturday. But it would be fine to have Mac teach her how to use it.

"Thanks," she replied to his offer as he opened the door to let Paddy hop into the vehicle and turned to lift Allison to the seat. He squeezed her hand in an absent-minded way when done. It settled in Allison as warm and familiar, before she recognized he probably automatically did that to his wife when she was alive. The warm fuzzy feeling disappeared like cotton candy on the tongue.

What was the matter with her? Only a month ago she had been engaged to Jack! *Am I fickle? Stupid? Shallow?* She didn't know, but she knew she was wary of her ex now.

Mac appeared solid and reliable, and she was attracted to him. Not just chemistry-wise. Though obviously some of that too, thinking back to how her body had reacted the first time she had seen him.

The attraction, different than the quick, fiery sensation in her blood around Jack, was thrilling yet comfortable, like she'd known him forever. It had to be squelched. It wasn't good for either of them. Her life had suddenly become dramatic and unsure. Or perhaps that had happened when she'd broken her engagement, instinctively fleeing to Wyoming because her gut intuition had said her former fiancé might be dangerous or had dangerous friends.

Mac pulled into a parking spot in front of the café. They had beat most of the other after-church diners.

Dressed in blue jeans and a white shirt with the signature white hat, he wasn't the suave New Yorker she was used to, but his courtesy of opening all doors for her, taking off his hat inside the café, and greeting everyone already there with his commanding presence still put him on the "I'm impressed" list she kept in her head.

She had started the list as a silly teenager, mentally recording her requirements for a husband. Jack had fit that list and look how wrong she'd been. She'd better delay putting this white-hatted animal doctor on it so soon.

The flavorful meatloaf Sunday Special, with real mashed potatoes, green beans with bacon pieces, and a small dish of chocolate pudding included, tasted like her mother's, and a pang of homesickness hit her.

So different than New York. Sunday dinner at a restaurant there had been expensive and ala carte. This was small-town country. Unpretentious. Comfortable. She liked it, and concentrated on enjoying her food, half-listening as Paddy filled her in on fishing and frog catching in the nearby creek.

Mac spent a lot of time studying her face, which she tried to ignore, giving him a small smile and a quick glance now and then. *Act natural. You can't let anyone know what might be happening with Jack. He might be dangerous. I'm sure he's gone. I'm safe. But I want a gun.*

When everyone was finished, Mac went up to the till to pay. She got up quickly, forgetting her sprained ankle, and twisted it as she turned from the table.

"Ooo!" came out too loud, and Mac was at her side in an instant.

"Are you okay? Did you hurt yourself?" He leaned down to peer at her face.

"I hurt my ankle a little," she said with a sharp intake of breath as a lightning bolt of pain streaked up her leg again. She grabbed his muscular forearm. "It'll be okay." She glanced around. She hated being the center of attention, but at least twelve pairs of eyes were trained on the two of them.

"Let's go," she said, clutching his muscled arm tenaciously, dragging him along and gritting her teeth against the aching soreness demanding notice with each step. She'd left her crutches in the pickup, not wanting to be a spectacle, like she'd just become.

"I'll take your other arm," Paddy loudly declared, not to be outdone by his dad.

"Thank you, Young Man," she smiled, then winced as she attempted to walk. *God, why this on top of Jack coming here?*

She spent an anxious afternoon after arriving home, readying lesson plans for school with part of her mind, listening for approaching vehicles or unusual sounds with the rest. Before going to bed, she checked that all windows were closed, and the door locked, and still couldn't close her eyes after she was under the covers.

How was she going to cope, cocooned in fear while trying to be a teacher? Maybe she should leave and move back to New York to be near her parents.

She shut her eyes and repeated the Lord's prayer, a favorite way to calm her thoughts allowing her to fall asleep. She apologized to God for interruptions to the familiar words as soft memories of Mac squeezing her hand and lifting her into his pickup dropped into the prayer.

After the Amen, a gust of wind rattled a window out in the living room. Sure it was the wind, she still needed to check. Perhaps it was the one Jack had crawled through when he "surprised" her with his visit. She shuddered with the fear he might be crawling through it again. Why had he pulled that weird stunt? It was a sneaky thing to do. And he was rarely sneaky. He liked being noticed, did everything with a public flourish if he could.

Carefully pushing the covers back, she lowered her feet to the floor, biting back an "Oof" as her injury protested. Managing a limping creep, she found the room empty and the window now silent, as if knowing she would reprimand it for being noisy. Her fanciful thought brought a small smile to her lips, until she thought of how she would act if she had a gun in her hand.

Could she shoot Jack if he came back?

CHAPTER FOURTEEN

With no emergency calls, Mac went to bed early, planning to catch up on sleep. However, sleep stayed out of reach until after midnight. Instead, scenes where he taught Allison to shoot a gun, which would surely necessitate putting his arms around her to help steady it, kept streaming on his brain's video screen. He saw her flaxen hair play with the breeze, as she squinted those vivid green eyes to aim...oh, he had the whole scene played out. And it would take many practice sessions to teach her, he was sure.

He drifted off with a smile on his face, continuing the lesson in dreamland, only to lose the smile when Jack waltzed into the dream, threw the weapon into a large sagebrush, and grabbing Allison's arm, hauled her off to his Porsche. He nodded off again, wondering if Jack still fit into the teacher's life. And if he mattered to her.

Mac took Paddy to school the next morning, feeling as sunny as the sky, hoping his favorite schoolmarm would be standing on the playground. He'd be cool and wave, then drive off. But he didn't have to act cool; she wasn't there.

"See you this afternoon," he motioned his son off. He'd quiz Paddy about the new teacher again when he got home. *Slow down. You're not a teenager. And she's got baggage, remember? Might not be a good idea to be so interested.* But the self-talk did nothing to decrease his heart rate, or his plans to spend more time with her. He pointed his truck toward the hardware store.

After ascertaining Dave did have several small pistols on sale that might be perfect for Allison, Mac returned to his ranchette and opened his clinic. His only excitement was vaccinating some feline pets early in the morning and getting slapped on the wrist by a sharp claw. He picked up the trade magazines that came in the mail the day before but couldn't concentrate on any of the articles.

Finally, giving into the desire that had been tickling his brain since breakfast, he decided to check Allison's yard out where he'd noticed the fresh-turned earth piled up. Maybe she'd seen it too and that's why she wanted a gun. Maybe she was afraid a bear would get her. Or a mountain lion. He grinned. Just like a woman.

Since it was mid-morning, he'd lunch at the café after his curiosity was satisfied. After driving to her house, Mac parked and tried the house door to make sure it was locked. Walking around back, he noted the tall, fall-dry, straw-colored grasses bent down in places like someone had walked there already. Maybe *not* a wild animal. Then he remembered the ex said he'd crawled in the back window to surprise "Allie," and he must have left his Porsche back there too. That's why he and Allison hadn't noticed Jack might be in the house when they returned from the dance.

Lines of pressed grass indicating vehicle tracks led to the old, weed-infested street behind the house. A wide path of flattened vegetation started where the car had sat and continued to the dirt pile. It looked like something had been dragged across the yard. He ambled closer.

The mound of soil was too big and too neat to have been made by an animal. No hole, so one had been dug and then filled again. Recently. All the dirt hadn't fit back into the hole so something else must have been put in there too. No weeds or plants grew on the diggings. It hadn't been packed down. Couldn't have been dug by anyone local...they'd have put the sod back on top.

He took off his hat and scratched his head, a habit when something puzzled him in the vet world. It showed people he was thinking hard, or so he hoped, and had started when he was young and inexperienced and wanted to look serious.

Why would someone dig a hole and fill it in again? No one usually bothered other people's lots in this small piece of civilization. This place was too isolated for her he thought.

He scanned the area, seeing only waving plants, and empty, abandoned yards. He needed a shovel.

After a round trip home for the shovel, and fifteen minutes of labor, he hit something soft. As he removed small chunks of soil, thinking perhaps someone had buried a pet there, a suit-coat sleeve with a hand protruding from it appeared and seemed to wave at him. A whoosh of air left Mac's chest. He could only stand open-mouthed with a shovelful of soil halted in mid-pitch. A body. He must be dreaming again.

Allison sighed as she shoved ungraded papers into her briefcase. The kids were gone. The lingering smell of twenty hot and sweaty fifth graders was dissipating. She closed the school room's windows against the warm air she'd let in earlier, hoping it would drop the temperature in the hotter, un-air-conditioned room. An exercise in futility—both her and the kids' concentration had melted in the heat. She trusted the new ventilation system being put in would be done soon.

She'd successfully kept Jack out of her head most of the day, Mac out of it another portion, and been able to truly focus on her students about half the day. *I'll have to do better*, she mused as she locked the classroom behind her.

She walked through the halls and left the school building a few minutes later, happy her mostly healed ankle allowed her to walk without crutches. She still wrapped it, however, and watched where she placed her foot. She could now drive without much discomfort.

Lifting her blonde ponytail off the back of her neck to cool it, and pursing her lips, she poofed at her bangs and gingerly touched the hot car door handle. Preoccupied with her thoughts, her burned fingers barely registered.

Like a loop recording, the memory of Jack's visit and odd behavior played continuously in the back of her mind. She concentrated on a crow being chased by a sparrow, a useless effort to get rid of the scenario. She'd make it through whatever happened somehow. And be okay.

She drove out of the school parking lot and adjusted the car's air conditioning to high. Remembering she meant to see if the hardware store carried guns, she turned toward Main Street.

A Highway Patrol car squealed around the highway turn-off and onto Main Street, increasing speed as it streaked past her. Having just gotten out of her car in front of Dave's Hardware, fine gravel spewed by its tires stung her ankles, and the resultant tepid whirlwind it stirred up ruffled her pony tail. She wrinkled her nose. Why weren't the streets paved? This is not New York, she reminded herself. And she was still glad for that.

She didn't know how many times a patrol whizzed through this small city, but she bet it wasn't often. People usually drove slowly in this western town of pickups and family SUVs. She hoped someone hadn't died or robbed the bank. She had planned to transfer one of her New York accounts here soon.

She looked through partially closed eyes in the bright sun, curious as to where the Patrol was heading, and observed it zoomed straight for her end of town. Her stomach dropped as a frisson of alarm began somewhere in her mid-section and rapidly spread to her head causing a short spurt of dizziness. Her heart started beating a rapid tat-tat against her breastbone.

'Scooting back in behind the steering wheel, she flung her purse onto the passenger seat and turned the ignition. A shiny black car with tinted windows flew past before she could back out into the street.

Movements jerky, she put her car in neutral, roared the motor, huffed over her mistake, and found reverse. Backing up, she spewed some gravel of her own as she turned toward her new home and hit the gas.

Jack. It had to be something to do with Jack. Wild possibilities marched through her mind. Had he come back? Killed himself? No, it couldn't happen. He was too much in love with himself to commit suicide. Killed Mac? A shaft of fear shot through her heart.

Her spirit sank as she neared her little house and realized the black car, a patrol car, the sheriff's vehicle, and Mac's truck, occupied her yard. Her breath caught on a sobbed "Oh, no" as she exited her car, left the door hanging open, and raced toward her house. Her eyes refused to focus, but she realized no one was in the house as, breathless, she rushed through, calling "Mac" every two seconds.

She heard voices coming from the back of her house. Peering through the gauzy curtain covering the windows, she saw several men standing in a circle between her house and the weedy back street. She turned and started to go back outside. A mewling cry tore from her throat as she forgot to be careful and twisted her previously injured ankle. Ignoring the pain, she reached for a crutch and limped outside.

Stumbling through the long grasses that snatched at her ankles and shoes, she rounded the corner to see Mac and two others in law enforcement uniforms standing beside a pile of dirt. The two in uniforms leaned on shovels. She then noticed two more men, in black business suits, walking the perimeter of her yard, studying the ground.

She headed over, reaching the cavity beside the dirt and stopped abruptly, losing her balance and tipping toward the sight in front of the men. Mac's hands grabbed her shoulders and pulled her back. A gasp escaped as she saw a man lying in the hollow.

"No!" she screamed. "No!" Her legs turned to jelly, and she fell backward into her veterinarian's arms. She turned and hid her face in his shirt.

*When has this man become **my** veterinarian? I don't have pets even.*

And with that irrational thought, she knew she was hallucinating. Else why would she be seeing Arnie, *dead,* in her backyard?

CHAPTER FIFTEEN

Mac cradled Allison in his arms, unsure how to feel. Had she known about the body in her yard? Could she have buried it, or did she know who had? Was Jack involved and was she covering for him? He really didn't know her, he reminded himself. She could be nothing more than a little liar. He, a gullible fool. But her reaction to seeing the body was genuine shock. He could see that. So he discarded the thought she might have buried it.

He'd immediately called the Sheriff when he'd discovered the body. And Sheriff Ramirez had called the FBI field office in Cheyenne, knowing Allison was from New York and the dead man could be too. He was dressed in a suit; there was no ID on him. The agents, who happened to be at the office in a rare happenstance, had made the 140-mile drive from Cheyenne immediately that afternoon, arriving at the scene shortly before Allison ended her school day. Now it looked like she was involved with something shady. He asked himself again if he should be entangled with someone like her.

"I want to go in the house," she mumbled into his shoulder.

"Ms. White," one of the two black-suited men standing near her said. "We need to ask you some questions." Both men opened small wallets with gold badges on one side and a picture labeled with large blue letters reading, "FBI" and "Special Agent" above it on the other side.

"My name is Drake, and this is my partner, Anderson. Do you know who is in the grave?"

Allison hid her face against Mac, her hands gripping his shirt. Little shards of fear tore through her body with each of the agent's words.

Calling the spot a grave sent ripples of panic through her. FBI agents asking her questions tightened her chest. She struggled to breathe.

How much should she say? If she told them what she knew about the man in the hole, would she be in danger? Was she anyway? What could this small-town veterinarian, whose image slid into her mind constantly now, be thinking? She was suddenly more afraid of that answer than being in danger from Jack.

She wished Mac would pick her up, tell her she was in a bad dream, and carry her away. His body was the only solid anchor in her world at this moment.

She drew back, stomped her feet to see if they'd hold her, winced at the pain in her right ankle, and let go of the fabric covering the man offering her tangible security. She felt bereft, and guilty, even though she knew there was nothing she was guilty of, except poor judgment in men.

She squinted at Agent Drake, his face backlit by the sun, keeping her from seeing his expression, and tried to summon forth saliva for her dry mouth.

"I...I don't actually know him. I met him...once...in New York." She still felt a certain amount of loyalty to Jack. She'd loved him. Could he have put Arnie here...in her backyard? No! Not the Jack she knew.

She looked aside, away from the body.

"Can we go in? Somewhere?" Her knees were going to buckle soon if she didn't sit down. She clutched her elbows with cold hands in an attempt to hold herself together. Even her voice quavered.

Mac's arm encircled her shoulders, warm, strong, and supportive.

"Sirs, let's go into the house. I think the lady needs to get off her feet. She has a sprained ankle." Mac gently guided Allison in a turn toward her home.

The two agents followed. She tried not to stumble, but her legs didn't seem to belong to her. She had to concentrate just to make them hold her up and move. Mac had handed her the crutch she'd dropped, and she leaned heavily on it, grasping it with both hands. Long stems of grass snagged her feet, further impeding her progress. She was in a horrible nightmare. She needed to wake up!

As they approached her entrance to the house, a sleek black hearse's tires crunched the gravel as it turned onto the little-used street behind her home.

A small whimper escaped her lips, and she closed her eyes, stumbling on her doorstep. Mac steadied her and assisted her over the sill then walked with her to the kitchen table, holding a chair out for her and not removing his hand from her elbow until she was seated.

After they were all seated, the FBI agents resumed the questions. "Now, Ms. White, it looked like you might have recognized the gentleman lying in your backyard, tell us how you might know him. Can you tell us his name?" Drake leaned toward her.

Scenes of the one night she'd interacted with Arnie tossed about in her brain like marbles in a tumbler. They'd sat next to each other, and he'd been attentive to her in ways that had made her uncomfortable, leaning near her when talking, looking at her sideways, often with a small smile on his face during the meal, making sure the waiter refilled her coffee as soon as he noticed her cup empty, laying his hand on her arm when conversing with her. Yet she'd never learned his last name. The woman, introduced as his wife, Wanda, had watched Allison closely with squinted eyes and a malevolent stare.

While she marshaled her thoughts, Anderson spoke.

"Ms. White? What can you tell us about the man in your backyard?"

"He...he was at a supper club my...my fiancé took me to in New York. He and his wife were at our table. I don't remember his last name if it was mentioned. But he was introduced to me as Arnie."

Should she tell him more? That he was Jack's friend? Or was he? She remembered the conversation in the ladies' room between the two women at her table.

She leaned forward. "How did he die? Did someone kill him?" She supposed that was a stupid question. She hadn't really seen anything but his face before she hid hers in Mac's shirt. If he died naturally, why would he have been buried in her yard? Had someone killed Arnie to frame Jack? Or had Jack killed Arnie?

"Ms. White," Drake said, "may I call you Allison? It appears he has a gunshot wound in his chest. We'll know more after the autopsy. Who were the other people there? In the restaurant. What is your fiancé's name?"

"He isn't my fiancé anymore. I mean, I broke our engagement. I came here...to Wyoming. We aren't engaged. I gave him his ring back." Her voice became more emphatic; it seemed important to get that fact across to the agents. "His name is Jack Corbel."

Everyone's eyes were trained on her. Her cheeks heated. The men's expressions appeared non-judgmental, just curious. But she'd watched detective shows. Wondered if they would start playing "bad cop/good cop" with her. It was all so nonsensical. And now their voices came through a blanket, or wall of cotton. And gray fuzz gathered around the edges of her vision.

Mac caught Allison as she toppled into his arms. Her eyes were closed, and her head lolled to one side. He scooped her up and headed for the worn-looking couch in her living room. He sensed the agents right behind him as he lowered her to the cushions. He quickly placed her feet on a throw pillow.

"Watch her!" he growled as he half-jogged to the bathroom to get a cold wet cloth. "Call 911!" he shouted at the one eyeing Allison speculatively.

"Can't this wait?" he demanded, returning to the room. "She has just had a terrible shock! She obviously didn't realize she had a body in her backyard." He laid the cold cloth on Allison's forehead and grabbed his cell phone, tapping the emergency button and giving Drake a frown for not following his orders. "Can we do this later, or tomorrow?"

"I'm sorry, sir, but the sooner the better. Please bring her down to the local police station when she recovers. We'll continue there." The two men disappeared through the door, leaving Mac standing beside an unconscious woman. Terrified, he yelled at the retreating figures.

"Hey wait! Can't you stay until she comes around? She might not come out of this!" He turned and knelt beside the inert form. The 911 call connected, and his heart constricted as he examined Allison's face for any sign she was coming to as he related her condition into the phone.

Still connected to the emergency call center, he pleaded in a soft voice. "Allison, wake up!" He rubbed her arm, rubbed her shoulder, listened for breath sounds.

Allison's eyes opened slowly, focusing on Mac. Her eyebrows raised.

"Mac? Why are you here? What happened?"

The men left. Mac's heart hammered at his chest wall. He reached for Allison's hands and searched her eyes. Was she okay? Did she have amnesia or something?

"You fainted. While the men were questioning you. Don't you remember?"

She was silent, staring at his face. As if she didn't understand. What was wrong with her? Sweat dampened his armpits. He'd never dealt with someone who wasn't right in her mind before. Or someone who had no memory.

CHAPTER SIXTEEN

Sirens announcing the arrival of an ambulance abruptly stopped as soon as they became deafening. Two people wearing green scrub suits with multiple pockets filled with small instruments burst into the house. Allison, sitting on the edge of her sofa, holding her head in her hands as if it might fall off and roll away, looked up as they approached.

"I'm okay, I'm okay," she sat up straight, dropping her hands to her lap as a blood pressure cuff encircled her arm and an oxygen sensor pinched her finger. Introductions happened quickly and simultaneously with checking her over.

Mac noted the dazed, puzzled look in her eyes, and kept shifting his positions to see around the ambulance attendants and examine her face.

"Can you take her to the hospital?" he questioned with a catch in his voice. He'd know what to do if she was a distressed heifer, but he hadn't had much experience with a distraught woman.

"No! I don't need the hospital! I just fainted, that's all. I'm okay, aren't I?" She turned her gaze to the male EMT. Tall and muscular, he looked more like a football hero than an EMT to Mac. But his hands were gentle as were the words he used to explain each task he did as he checked her over. He'd introduced himself as Lane. His partner, named Bev, was a petite woman who stood by ready to assist if needed.

"Your blood pressure's within normal range, your pulse is settling and your oxygen's good. Are you sure you don't want to come in for further testing?" Lane asked.

"No. No, I'm fine. I just had a shock. Thanks, thanks for coming...for checking on me. Do you need information from me or something? My insurance card? How do I pay for this?"

"Just stop in at the hospital business office tomorrow, ma'am. We'll get your information then. We're just glad you're okay," Lane reassured.

"We'll be going then." He turned to his partner. "Let's pack it up, Bev." They disappeared through the door as suddenly as they'd come.

Mac sank down beside Allison on the couch. "We have to go down to the police station. Are you sure you're up to it? How well did you know that guy in the grave?" The question shot out his mouth like a calf suddenly freed from a corral. He sensed she knew more about the dead man than she'd told the authorities. He knew he shouldn't have asked at that moment, but his curiosity was eating a hole in him. *What kind of woman is she? And why do I care?* He sent up a bullet prayer—*Guide me, Lord. Am I supposed to be here? Doing this? Attracted to her? Looking out for her? Am I crazy?*

Mac was afraid God would answer yes to the last question he'd asked Him as he helped Allison stand and walk to his vehicle with a hand at her elbow. But the pull to be with her remained strong. He hadn't felt an attraction like that since Catherine. But Catherine hadn't come with baggage. She'd been sweet, uncomplicated, and embraced the same values he did—honesty, not subterfuge, a simple ranching family background, not big city sophistication.

Allison settled on the passenger seat of his truck as he rounded the hood. She hadn't responded to his questions. But, sooner or later he'd get answers. He wasn't going any further in his relationship with this complicated city gal until he found out a few more things about her. Or so he told himself.

Allison glanced around as she entered the police station. She'd never been in one in New York but figured it wouldn't have looked like this one—with a dingy front entrance room void of decorations and a high counter featuring only a pencil lying on it. A closed door behind the counter sported a sign stating, "Personnel Only." Somehow, she felt guilty and soiled just walking into the room.

"Right this way, Ms. White," Agent Drake had appeared from a side entrance. He was back to being formal as if they'd never met at a grave, and he hadn't established he could call her Allison. It must be some psychological ploy used in questioning her.

A local officer emerged from an office at the back of the room, leaving the door open, showing a desk littered with papers, in and out boxes, both full, and two hard wooden chairs with arms in front of it. She followed the black-suited man in, grateful Mac stayed close beside her.

"Have a seat, Ms. White...Dr. MacFadden." Drake gestured to the hard seats as he sat in a cushioned one to face them with the desk between them. She again noted bare walls except for some official documents in frames that made no sense to her disordered thoughts.

"Would you like a glass of water?"

"Yes, please, if you don't mind." She hated that her voice came out small and hesitant, like that of a child. She had walked without thinking to the innermost chair placed in a corner in front of the desk, with Mac sitting between her and the outlet. She now felt trapped and gripped the chair arms as a moment of claustrophobia struck. She took three deep breaths as she normally did when she started losing control of a classroom.

An assistant appeared and handed her a glass of water. She raised both hands to hold it and took a grateful sip, then set it down carefully, afraid she'd drop it from her nervous fingers.

Drake grabbed a form from a briefcase beside him. He wrote a date on it. She stared at his blue tie patterned with black lines crossing each other. Something neutral to calm her jumping insides.

"May I have your full name and address, Ms. White?" The common questions of occupation, start date of job, etc. eased some of her discomfort. She produced her driver's license, glad Mac had thought to grab her purse and bring it. Then the questioning turned serious.

"Now, Ms. White, can you tell us anything more you might know about the body we found in your yard."

She wished he hadn't said body. Why not say man? But then he might have said "dead man" and that would have been just as bad.

She looked up, noting her questioner had round cheeks, probably from too many donuts, she thought insanely. A knot of panic bubbled up in her throat. She couldn't swallow. This was a dream, a nightmare. She managed to pull in a deep breath and looked at Mac. Did she see suspicion in his eyes?

She studied her lap. She needed to find her mojo, as the kids called it. Tense and stick-like, she leaned forward, raising her eyes and stabbing a look at the agent's eyes.

"I told you. I met him once...in New York. I...I was out to dinner with my fiancé and Arnie, that's his name, was there too, with a woman...his wife. That's all I know." Her microburst of irritation and courage evaporated.

She turned toward Mac again, her eyes pleading with him to believe her. His brows were furrowed, his ice-blue eyes still trained on hers. Did he think she lied? Panic beat like a drum in her chest, her stomach, her head.

"It's true," she added more to him than the man on the other side of the desk.

"Do you have a last name for this Arnie, Ms. White?" Her interrogator leaned slightly toward her, folding his hands together as if praying. Allison wished she could pray right now. She was two people, one struggling to answer the authorities, the other removed from the scene and knowing it was just a nightmare.

"You can call me Allison."

"Do you know his last name?" He softened his voice and unclasped his hands, poising a pen over a form in front of him.

"No, I only met him once." How many times would she have to repeat herself?

Do you know the name of the woman who was with him? His wife?"

"Wanda, her name was Wanda."

"What did you talk about? Did Arnie and his friends mention what kind of work they did?"

"No!" Allison's response came out sharper than intended. The room was getting stuffy and she struggled to inhale. Why couldn't they leave her alone and just go after whomever they wanted? She wasn't connected to these people anymore. She left them when she left New York. *But you are still connected,* a little urchin in her head inserted. *Arnie was dead in your backyard.*

"Can you tell us your fiancé's full name and where your fiancé is now?" The brown eyes of Agent Drake stared intently at her again.

"I don't know where he is. He's not my fiancé anymore. He's gone." She moistened her dry lips. She forgot she'd made up her mind not to say he'd been to her place in Sage Flats. "I told you his name is Jack Corbel. He's from New York."

"He's gone. So, he was here? In Sage Flats? For how long? How long ago? When did he leave?" His eyes squinted, peering right into her soul.

"He..." How much should she say? Should she even be protecting her ex? What if he was the murderer?

"Ms. White, withholding evidence in a homicide case can cause you to be charged with obstructing justice. Can you tell me your fiancé's full name—first, middle, and last—and where he is now?"

"I told you. Jack Corbel. I don't know where he is now. I guess I don't know if he has a middle name." She looked at the floor. She had been so starved to fall in love, she had planned to marry a man without knowing if he had a middle name.

"When did he leave?" The agent's words were enunciated so distinctly, she knew he was losing patience with her, and probably felt she was hiding something.

Mac's hand reached over and loosened one of hers from the chair arm, keeping it encased in his. "Tell him everything you know, Allison, if Jack is in danger from someone, you may be helping him. If he's not in trouble, you have nothing to fear from telling Agent Drake what you know."

Tears made Mac's face wavy as she examined his expression. His warm hand cradling hers conveyed caring to her icy cold one. She cleared her throat.

"I don't know for sure where he is. He left here last Saturday. I wanted him to leave. He became angry." Once she started, the words poured out of her, releasing a river of dread. "I broke our engagement before I moved here. I decided he wasn't right for me. I was afraid." The final admission slid out without permission.

"What were you afraid of, Allison?" The agent's voice quieted, conveying sympathy and inviting confidentiality. While her mind resented his technique, she still responded.

"His friends made me uncomfortable. I...I think he might have been involved with some scary people. He might not have known what kind of people they were," she hastened to assure. "But things seemed uncertain. And I thought I should end the engagement. He came here wanting to resume it. I didn't, and he got mad at me."

Mac squeezed her hand and laid it on her knee, withdrawing his as he did so, as if he'd gotten her to say what he knew the interrogator wanted and was removing his support. She felt abandoned.

"Can you tell us what kind of car Mr. Corbel was driving? And what his last known address was?" Drake was back to being business-like. Allison marveled when Mac broke into the conversation, recited the license plate numbers and said it was a black Porsche. She hadn't realized he'd noticed. But then, every guy notices a Porsche. Jack brought the subject of his *Porsche* into every conversation he could.

"Do you know his address in New York, Allison?" Drake repeated when she didn't answer right away.

Reluctantly, she told him. "Are you going to look for him?" she asked, feeling somehow in danger if Jack knew what she'd told them. But then why should it be wrong if he had done nothing criminal? *But what if he is guilty? Of murder? Will he hurt me?*

"We would like to talk to him. Maybe he can help solve our mystery. You can go home now, Ms. White, but don't leave town. And please, call us if you have any more information or Mr. Corbel comes back to visit you," Drake said. His arm stretched across the desk with a small card extended between his fingers.

The agent's voice had become merely background noise while her mind conjured up reasons to be terrified, but the business card being handed her drew her back to the moment as she understood they were dismissed, for now.

She hadn't told the agents about the conversation she'd overheard in the bathroom between the two women, as if keeping quiet about it lessened the meaning it might have in Arnie's death. Anything might incriminate Jack. But why was she hesitant to implicate him? Was it just fear? She didn't fully understand herself. And a new dread gripped her. *Am I withholding evidence?*

Mac and Allison rose, his hand gravitating to her waist as he allowed her to precede him out of the office. It caused a comforting yet exciting tingle of energy to invade her stomach, and she was surprised she noted it with fear and guilt running circles in her brain.

There existed a connection to this handsome, small-town vet, one she couldn't explain. It made her feel safe...cared for. A force drawing them together was almost palpable, and she didn't want to resist. She thought he felt it too.

They walked, without speaking, through the cooling late afternoon breeze to Mac's truck, and as they drove away, he asked, "Would you like to stay at our place tonight so you're not alone? Or I could park outside your house. But at my place, if I get called out during the night, you'd be with my housekeeper and son. I can take you home to pick up what you might need for a night or two, then take you back with me. Or you can follow me in your car. I live about a half mile out of town, opposite end from you. Lots of prairie around my place—wide open space. You can see anyone coming from a long ways away. The only things that sneak up on us are skunks and prairie dogs." He glanced her way with a smile.

Did he mean it? It felt like a lifeline, but should she bother him with her troubles? Would Jack come back? Was she in danger? Surely not. She didn't want to bring harm to him or Paddy. But she noted the sun getting dangerously close to the horizon and wondered how safe she'd feel when darkness closed in.

"Are you sure?"

"Yeah," he answered. "Paddy would love it if his favorite teacher came to stay with us. And...I would too," he added softly. "We can let the PD know where you are in case something else turns up."

"Thank you. I really don't have to if it's an imposition. But, I guess, I would feel...better." She stumbled over expressing her feelings. She still felt a need to deny Jack might be involved in a murder and called herself a coward for doing so.

CHAPTER SEVENTEEN

"You can have Paddy's room, and he can bunk with me." Mac led her to a bedroom in his home adorned with posters of baseball greats, and a bookcase filled with model cars and trucks. A handmade quilt pieced out of material featuring different sports covered the twin-sized bed. It was a perfect little boy's room.

"I can't uproot Paddy."

"He'll love it." Mac was still not sure he did the right thing by inviting her there, but the invitation had just jumped out of him. He needed to know she was okay, keep her safe. He was drawn to her even when he wasn't physically near her. He wondered if she felt it too. "Paddy will feel special having you here, and he loves to crawl into bed with me when he can. I mean to enjoy it before he becomes a teenager who holes up in his room and doesn't speak to me."

"If you're sure..." she took a tentative step into the room.

"Sure," Mac said as he pushed Paddy's clothes to one side of the closet. "Hang your items here. You'll have to share the bathroom with Paddy and me. I hope you don't mind. I'll let Mrs. Thompson know you're a guest here for a short time. She'll put fresh bedding on for you.

"Paddy's probably out playing with his horse. I'll tell him he gets to sleep with me tonight. Is there anything else I can get you right now?" He took a deep breath and pushed it out slowly through pursed lips, shaking his hands to get rid of the tension curling his fingers.

"Supper is at 6:30. Come into the kitchen and I'll introduce you to my housekeeper, Mrs. Thompson." Was he repeating himself? Was this the thing to do? Questions circled his brain.

He felt edgy. Why shouldn't he be? He had just brought a relative stranger home to stay in his son's room. One who might be a murderess. Whatever prompted him to do so? Or her to accept?

Things weren't going the way Allison had envisioned—moving to a sleepy cow town and hiding out in the sagebrush in the middle of nowhere. That's what she'd told her image in the mirror she'd be doing when deciding to leave New York. She'd barely arrived, and she was involved in a murder, had met someone who made her heart skip beats, had visited the local ER, and was a guest of the local veterinarian because she was afraid to go to her own home.

She had noted his act of shaking his tension out, she'd done it many times herself. So, she knew he was now questioning his offer of hospitality. She should leave. But she stood and felt the way her heart thumped just looking at him. And couldn't make herself go. She preceded him to the brightly lit kitchen, into a cloud of seasoned smells.

Supper provided a congenial atmosphere for getting acquainted with Regina Thompson, the housekeeper who lived with the family, and to answer the many questions Paddy had stored up for her. Mac remained silent after beginning the meal with a short prayer, thanking God for the food, the friendship, and His care that day.

"Did you live on a ranch? Do you have a horse?" Paddy asked first.

"I grew up in a big city, I never even had a cat," she smiled across the table at the young boy who looked to have a hard time sitting still as he stabbed a piece of meat on his plate. "I was busy playing with my dolls, taking ballet lessons, and going to school. I took ice skating lessons when I was your age. But we didn't have animals, I've only seen animals in the zoo and on TV. You'll have to educate me about horses. I hear you have one. What's it like? What did you name it?"

"His name is Buddy. 'Cause he's my buddy when I'm home. I don't have any brothers and sisters, do you?"

"No, just me. Would you like brothers and sisters?" The question skipped out before she thought of the ramifications of asking. She glanced at Mac who was staring at the wall with a stony look on his face.

"Um-huh," Paddy nodded. "But Dad says he'd have to get married for that. My mom died a couple years ago, and I never had any brothers, but I want one. Sisters are pests, Greg says." Allison saw Mac grimace. She couldn't seem to keep her eyes off him. She struggled to concentrate on his son.

"I remember Mom playing with me a lot though. But sometimes she spanked me. I remember her holding me and singing to me when I had a stomachache too. That's a nice memory, isn't it?" Eager blue eyes looked to Allison for approval.

"It is...and it sounds like your mom loved you. Moms have to spank sometimes and hug sometimes. That's a good mom," she smiled. She wondered how much love and sorrow Mac still held for his late wife, and how she'd died.

"Now tell me more about your horse." Struggling to keep focus on her small informant, she wanted to steer the conversation back to something neutral.

"He's cool! Want to come see him? Dad, can I take Ms. White out to the barn to see Buddy?"

Mac nodded. "Sure, good idea, I'll come along too. It's getting dark out. Regina, that was a great meal. Thanks."

Everyone rose from the table and Allison turned to thank Mrs. Thompson too, and was disconcerted when the lady smiled and thanked her back for sharing the meal, then reached over to hug her neck, and gave her a peck on the cheek. She found she liked the informality even as she drew back from it. Where she came from, even a friend just kissed the air beside her ear as a greeting.

"I'm so glad you are here, Ms. White. Please let me know if I can get you anything to make your stay more comfortable."

Her eyes inexplicably wet, Allison nodded. "Call me Allison, please. I will."

Wearing a pair of comfortable but expensive flats from a designer shoe store in New York City, Allison was thankful a smooth path to the barn didn't stress her sprain, and the middle floor of the barn was swept clean. She'd never been in a barn before and hadn't known what to expect. The scents of hay and horse greeted her, tickling her sinuses. She sneezed.

"Whoa," Mac said. "You're not allergic to horses, are you?" He tilted his head to peer at her from under his hat brim.

"Not that I know of. These are just new smells to me. Oh!" She stumbled back as a large horse's head popped out of a stall over a half-door right in front of her. Mac's warm hands grabbed her shoulders, steadying her. She wanted them to stay there, but he dropped them.

"That's Dad's horse," Paddy was quick to begin the tour. "His name is Bill. Isn't that a funny name for a horse?" Paddy looked at her grinning. She struggled to concentrate on Paddy's conversation.

"And over here," he walked to an adjoining paddock, "is Buddy! Come on, come over here. Pet him. He's really friendly."

Allison circled around Bill's head and approached the smaller head of Buddy, also stretching out over a half-door and examining Paddy's hand.

"He thinks I've got a treat for him, don't you, boy?" he said, rubbing the pony's nose. "He's been my horse since I was seven," he stood taller as he spoke. "I can ride him whenever I want. Sometimes I ride up into the hills, looking for snakes," he bragged.

Allison looked at Mac, surprised he would let such a small boy go by himself into this western wilderness.

Mac laughed. "He's not allowed to go off my property alone," he said in a low voice. "But I let him take the lead when we go up into those red buttes, and he feels pretty important then." The pride he had in Paddy shone in his eyes.

Reassured, she turned back to the little cowboy, as she now thought of him. "That must be kind of fun and scary!"

"Yeah, but I'm careful. Sometimes Dad rides with so he can shoot the snakes if he has to. I can't shoot a gun yet," his voice became soft and thoughtful. "But next year I'm going to join 4-H and take a gun safety class!"

"What's 4-H?" Allison asked.

"It's a cool club, where you can learn to shoot bows and arrows, and raise cows and sheep and do all kinds of things, then you can enter them in the fair and win prizes and everything!" Obviously, he couldn't wait.

"Dad!" Paddy shouted as he ran to look out the barn door. "We've got company!"

Allison froze as she and Mac walked outside and saw two men in black suits get out of a shiny red Corvette parked by a bright yard light.

CHAPTER EIGHTEEN

"Mac." Allison put her hand on his arm. "Who are they?"

"I thought maybe you'd know." His glance and tone of voice were hard as he looked at her.

"Me? Why would I know?" But she sensed danger, making her voice weak. It had to be something to do with Jack, or Arnie. These men had to be from New York. They could be Mafia.

"Hi, folks," Mac's voice was friendly as they all met in the middle of the yard, Paddy sticking close to his dad's leg. "I'm Dr. MacFadden. How can I help you?" He smiled. The outside light on the barn and the glow from the sunset helped illuminate the two strangers' faces in the growing darkness.

Allison's face stiffened, she pressed her lips together hard and clasped sweaty hands behind her back. She felt as if the hair on the back of her neck was standing up. The men's gazes focused on her as they reached to shake Mac's hand.

"We are looking for a friend of ours who said he was headed out this way. Since we were passing through, thought we'd stop and see if he found what he was coming here for, and maybe visit. We asked around town and some people talked about a body being found in the new teacher's backyard. Someone saw the new teacher drive out of town with the doctor here, so thought we'd stop by and say hello. Thought you might be acquainted with our friend."

They still hadn't introduced themselves, but their eyes were pinned on her face. They wanted to find Jack and were fishing for information. Would they believe her when she said she didn't have a clue where Jack had disappeared to? She could see in their faces they already knew of her relationship with him.

"Who...who are you looking for?" She hated that her voice halted mid-sentence, indicating her fear while playing their game.

"Aren't you Jack Corbel's fiancée? Jack said you came out for a retreat here, and he was coming out to get you. We thought we'd just stop by and say 'Hi'. Does he know you got another interest out here too?" The taller of the two, who had black hair sticking out under a partially pushed-back black hat, grinned as he asked. She looked into his eyes and saw...nothing, no emotion or friendliness. He would have been handsome except for a rather bulbous nose flattened in its center, and the mocking grin.

"I don't know where Jack is." She firmed her voice. "He was here, but he left. Jack and I have broken up. I'm not going to marry him anymore. So, he's gone. A couple days ago. I'm sorry, he's not *here*!"

She darted a look at the second man whose hat was pulled low over his eyes. He was staring at her. The muscle in his cheek rippled. Goosebumps lifted the hair on her arms.

"So that *wasn't* him in your backyard? We were told by some of your friends in town, it might be someone named Arnie. Is that who was in your backyard? He was a friend of ours too. How would he end up in your backyard?" The second man's deep voice wasn't friendly sounding. She felt accused of something. Her feet froze to the ground. These men knew so much. She didn't know how to answer, she just wanted to run back to the house and hide. Mac laid his hand on her shoulder as if he sensed her panic.

"You sure you didn't hear Jack say where he was going?" bulbous nose brought her attention back to him.

The cheek clencher spoke with a Bronx accent, "Ma'am, we got some news for our friend, see, and it's important we find him soon. We drove a long ways out of our way to locate him. You sure you don't know where he is?"

"I...I don't!" Allison took a prolonged breath. She had to control her anxiety. "He and I quarreled. He left, and I don't expect him back. I'm sorry."

"Okay, ma'am," bulbous nose said. "We'll check back when we come through this way again. Not sure when though. Small town here, we'll find you. So don't worry about getting back to us if you hear from Jack. We'll be in touch."

He touched his hat brim and the two turned in tandem and walked back to their car. The last statement sounded like a threat. Allison grabbed Mac's arm with both hands, clutching it like it was a lifeline.

"Can we go in now?" she asked, her voice breathless. Her knees were turning to jelly.

"What was that all about?" Mac asked as he sat across the kitchen table from her. Paddy stood by his shoulder, mouth open and eyes intent on her face.

"I've never seen them before. They have to be..." she glanced at Paddy, so much more innocent than the ten-year-olds of New York, "Well, you realize who they might be, don't you?" She raised green eyes to look into Mac's blue ones and forgot her caution in front of the young boy. "I don't understand what's going on! I don't know who killed Arnie! This is frightening me!"

Mac's inclination was to take her in his arms. But was she as innocent as she claimed? Should she be teaching fifth grade in Sage Flats? Teaching his son?

"Are bad guys after you?" Paddy's eyes opened wide, and he came to her side. "Why are you scared, Ms. White? Don't be scared. Dad and I will look out for you, won't we Dad?"

"It's okay." He needed to calm her and move Paddy away from her. "It will be okay. We'll figure it out. Why don't you get ready for bed, Paddy, and I'll come and read you a story. Get your jammies out of your room so Ms. White can go in there later. You can crawl into my bed after you brush your teeth. You got school tomorrow so better hop to it, Son. Go now." He gave Paddy a push toward the hall.

"But, Dad, it's early!" Paddy gave his usual response, drawing out the "early," but distracted from his questions as his dad intended.

"No, it's time. You go now. I'll be along after a moment. Go now!" Mac bit back his frustration with Paddy.

He turned back to Allison and saw fear in her eyes. The urge to pull her into his lap and surround her with his arms was so strong, his hands began to rise on their own. He purposely put them down on top of his thighs.

"Have you ever seen those two guys before?" He couldn't keep the suspicion from his voice.

"N...no!" She stared at him. "Don't you believe me? Why would I lie?"

"I'm sorry. It's just that we've never had stuff like this happen in Sage Flats in the fifteen years I've lived here. We're so far removed from big-city crime...I'm having trouble getting my mind around all this!" He gestured with his hands. "How did that body end up in your backyard?"

"I don't know," she said, and immediately burst into tears. Mac gave into his impulse and reaching for her hand, tugged her over onto his knees, wrapping her and his doubts in his arms as she wet his shirt again with her waterworks.

A few minutes later, she slid off his lap and snatched a napkin from the table, blotting her eyes and sniffing.

"I'm sorry. I...thank you...for being so nice. You," she slanted him a look, "you are very kind, I...I better go to bed. Please forgive me for crying on your shirt again." She turned toward Paddy's bedroom and fled.

Allison closed the door to the small room and plopped down on the bed. Torturing the napkin still in her hand, she tried to sort through myriad confusing thoughts—the feel of Mac's arms around her, the horror of the image of Arnie in the shallow grave, the skeptical looks of Agent Drake and Mac, Paddy's ready and simple acceptance of her in their home. Drained of all energy, she lay down on her side, pulled an afghan lying at the foot of the bed over her shoulders, and slept.

CHAPTER NINETEEN

Morning was usually a bit of a trial for Mac and Paddy. The habit of getting up, eating breakfast without complaint, and getting ready for school on time had to be relearned each day. But Allison being there was apparently motivation enough for Patrick to arrive early at the table.

Mrs. Thompson was serving pancakes to Allison when the two males arrived. Mac glanced at her and saw the pale complexion emphasized by darker circles cradling her eyes.

"Good morning, Ms. White. You beat me! I was fast this morning, but Dad made me take a shower, or maybe I could have beat you!" Paddy chattered. "Do you want to go see Buddy after breakfast? I probably should go give him some hay, anyway." He puffed out his chest like a small rooster and Allison's smile encouraged him further.

"We can go out as soon as we're done eating if we hurry, can't we, Dad?"

Mac, intent on watching Allison's face and attempting to work out his puzzling feelings, didn't hear the plea.

"Dad? Dad, are you listening?" Paddy persisted. "We can go see Buddy, can't we?"

The question remained unanswered as the phone on the kitchen counter jangled, and Allison jumped, staring at it as if a boogeyman lived inside. Yesterday's memories had rushed at her as soon as she'd awakened and she felt ready to jump out of her skin. Mac kept his gaze on her as he left the table to answer it.

"Hello" was followed by a short pause, then a loud "Who is this?" A moment later he replaced the receiver.

"Paddy, if you're done eating, go brush your teeth and meet me in the truck!"

"But, Dad! I asked if I can show Ms. White how I feed Buddy!"

"Now! I want you to go brush your teeth and get your books and *meet me in the truck!*" he repeated.

"Come on, Paddy," Mrs. Thompson put her hand on his shoulder. "Let's talk about it while you clean those teeth. Perhaps, Ms. White doesn't have time before school." Paddy glanced back with a hurt look on his face as he followed the housekeeper.

As soon as Mac and Allison were alone, he sat down beside her. "That was Wanda."

"Wanda! Arnie's wife?" Allison's eyes widened and she gripped the edge of the table. "What would she want? I only met her that one time!" Her voice rose, and she stood.

Mac stood too, laying warm hands on her cold shoulders and pulling her against his chest, shushing her and laying his cheek on the top of her head as her cheek lay against him. It felt so natural to hold her. He wondered if she could hear his heart speed up at her nearness. He hesitated to tell her about the call and end the moment.

"She said she knew you and what kind of person you are. And she sort of threatened you."

"Threatened me?" Her voice scaled the high keys.

"She said she will do what she has to so everyone knows how you killed him." He tightened his arms when he felt her trembling.

She reared back and looked at him. "Killed him!" Her vocal execution was at the top of the scale now. "What does she mean, I killed him? I didn't kill Arnie. I didn't even know he was in my backyard! Or for how long!" Her body wilted, and Mac slipped his arms under hers to hold her up.

"Sh-sh. It's okay. We'll figure out where she got that idea. We have to talk to the police. I'll take you. It will be okay," he repeated. He had no idea if he could deliver on that promise, but he wanted to tamper down the hysteria that seemed to be rising.

Paddy came bounding into the kitchen and skidded to a stop. His eyes grew big as he blurted, "Dad! Why are you hugging Ms. White again? Is she sick?"

"Yes," he improvised. "I have to take her to see someone. Mrs. Thompson will have to take you to school today. We'll call in that Ms. White is sick, and they'll find a substitute for her."

He reached for the phone as Paddy backed out of the room still staring at Allison as she slid out of Mac's arms and onto a chair.

Allison felt boneless. She was no killer. Why would Wanda call and make such an accusation? She supposed the police had informed Wanda about Arnie's death and the circumstances, where they'd found him, and that was how Wanda found out where she was. Had the two men who'd visited last night told her whose house she was at? But what did that mean for her? She needed her dad.

Mac returned to her side, and she looked into his face. She saw concern, but also doubt and confusion. She didn't blame him. She had her own doubts and confusion. He took her hands and said, "Come on. We need to talk to the police about this."

She got up and followed, still clinging to one of his hands. She had no will of her own right then. She couldn't even pray.

"Will...will you pray for me?" She looked at Mac's face and saw his eyebrows lift in surprise. "I wouldn't know what to say...for myself, I mean. I need someone to do it for me. Could you?" Her voice broke on the last request, and a tear forged a crooked path down her cheek.

Mac's warm thumb brushed it away, as his hands cupped her face, and he leaned close. "Yes," he said as he planted a fatherly kiss on her forehead.

Grabbing her hands, he closed his eyes. *Father, You understand what's happening and why. But, since we don't, please give us peace and strength, knowing You have everything under control, and will be with*

Allison as she figures this out. Give her insight and wisdom. Calm her fears and let her be aware You are with her. Amen."

"Let's go now. The sooner the better."

Feeling braver but bereft as he dropped her hands, her forehead tingled where the kiss still lay.

CHAPTER TWENTY

The FBI agents had remained in Sage Flats, and it was Drake who ushered Mac and Allison into the tiny, cluttered office again, steepling his hands as he faced them from behind the scarred wooden desk when they were all seated.

"You remembered something?" he asked, his gaze intent on Allison's face.

"What? No! I...I have been threatened...by...by someone. But I didn't do it! I don't even know how this disaster started! I'm not a killer!" Her emotions frayed, like multiple strings being pulled apart. Anger, fear, hurt and the compulsion to scream all vied for expression. Her hands fluttered in the air as she spoke, echoing her inner chaos.

She repeated Wanda's call and message to her, leaning toward him to show her earnestness.

"I only saw Wanda and Arnie once! At that dinner! And I broke up with Jack shortly after that. I can't even perceive why she would do this to me!"

Mac reached over and covered one of her cold hands with his sheltering, warm hand. She curled her fingers through his.

"How did she know where to call?" Sergeant Drake asked.

"Allison, tell Drake about the visit by those two thugs yesterday," Mac said.

The agent sat up straighter. "Two thugs?"

She related the drop-by of the two men looking for Jack. Her palms sweated and she let go of Mac's hand to rub them on her slacks. She had to be having a nightmare.

"If you are keeping an eye on me, didn't you see them? Are you protecting me or not?" Her voice gained volume. "Do I need an attorney?"

"You might want to get one on board just in case," the FBI agent said. "But at this point, you are not charged with anything, nor do

I know that you will be. However, you are involved in what has happened. We will keep an eye on your whereabouts and anyone coming into town to visit you. The investigation is between us and the FBI field office in New York. We keep the police informed here also. If you cannot reach me or my partner, please call them. They have given us this office to use while we are here, but we may have to leave at times. Where are you staying?"

"She'll stay with me," Mac said. "We won't leave her alone.

Mac looked at Allison and saw her lower lip quiver. Her eyes, wide open with large pupils, told him she was either going into hysteria or shock. How could he feel so connected to her when he didn't truly know her? He experienced familiarity when he touched her, a completeness he hadn't known for a long time when she was beside him. How ridiculous! He chided himself. She was almost a stranger, an attractive stranger, but still, merely an acquaintance at this point.

He cupped her elbow to help her stand and guide her out of Sergeant Drake's office. She stumbled as she walked and he had the strongest desire to sweep her up into his arms and carry her out to the vehicle, just like he'd done on the dance floor when he first met her. A senseless primal urge.

He helped her into the pickup and heard the sob as he slammed the door shut. He whipped it open again and leaned into the cab, catching her as she fell against him. Helpless, he held her as she sobbed into his shoulder. Something in his chest pulled tight, an emotion he couldn't name. He found himself kissing the top of her head and laying his cheek on her silky hair.

"Ah, Colleen," he murmured, not realizing he called her by the pet name he'd had for Catherine. "It'll be all right," he whispered. "We'll make it all right, things will sort themselves out, you'll see."

Her sniffling stopped and she straightened and turned toward the dash, wiping her nose with a tissue she drew out of her purse.

Allison went into Paddy's room and closed the door when they got back to his house. He should leave her be; he was sure she had some thinking to do. But the pull was strong to follow her and take her in his arms again. He had obviously lost his reasonable objectivity where this big-city girl was concerned. He was afraid he was losing his heart too.

Allison sank onto the bed and lay with her head on the pillow. She was exhausted physically and emotionally. How could life be such a mess? She sensed Mac was outside the door wondering about the whole situation, most likely sure he was now sorry he had ever linked himself in any way to such a crazy, troublesome woman. She was in his house and not a good influence on his son. She would have to leave.

But she also wanted to open the door and ask Mac to hold her again. She didn't understand why she felt so drawn to him. She barely knew him, and she was certainly fickle to not want to part from someone she hardly knew when she recently thought she was in love with Jack Corbel. What kind of person was she? Pondering that, she fell asleep.

CHAPTER TWENTY-ONE

Allison showed up for school the following morning with makeup repairing the look of not enough sleep and too much stress on her face. The blotchy effects of crying had faded to almost skin tone and her liquid foundation covered a multitude of sins. Mascara on her spiky lashes accentuated her green eyes. She needed her makeup on to tell her she was in control of herself and her life. At least she looked put together on the outside. Shallow of her, but it worked for now.

She knew she had decisions to make at the end of the day. She couldn't stay in limbo. She avoided the lunchroom at noon by sitting in her car by herself. She wasn't ready to discuss any of her latest life crises with anyone, not even Penny, yet.

She managed to conduct her classroom with some sense of normalcy, for herself and her students. Not until the final bell did she dwell on why she should leave Mac's place, yet she didn't want to go back to her rented house knowing Jack might return. She needed to talk to someone. Her decision solidified when she spied her friend Penny walking by her door.

"Penny!" She started for the door, and they almost collided as Penny came through in response to Allison's call.

"What, Allison? What's wrong? Your voice sounds funny. They said you called in sick yesterday. And I couldn't find you at lunch today."

"I...I have to talk to you about something. And maybe get some advice from you. Are you free for a few minutes?"

"Sure! Want to talk in here? Go out for pie? Come over to my place?"

"Can we go to your place? I need somewhere private. Are you ready to leave?"

"In ten minutes. Meet you at my apartment. Are you okay to drive there?"

Penny had picked up on her nervousness. Maybe she hadn't fooled her students either, although she hoped so. She didn't want kids telling their parents their new teacher was flaky.

"I'm okay. See you there."

Allison sat in a cushioned, rolling dining chair that encouraged relaxation at Penny's apartment, and responded by scooting to its edge and leaning forward. She was in no mood to relax.

"Penny, I have to tell you something about my life in New York and what's happening here. You may not want to be my friend after you hear."

She poured out what she knew about Jack, her broken engagement, and being accused by Wanda of killing Arnie, adding that Mac said she could stay at his place for safety, but she wasn't sure if she should.

"Oh, Allison! How awful for you! I heard about the body in your backyard of course. The whole town has. I was shocked! I tried to call your house but didn't get an answer. And your cell phone went right to voicemail. I didn't want to keep calling or come over if you were sick. I wondered if it just might be nerves. What are you going to do? How can I help?" Penny leaned toward her and grabbed both of Allison's hands. "I will pray for you, but what else can I do? Do you need a place to stay? I have a futon you can use. It might be crowded in this small apartment, but I wouldn't mind if you wouldn't. However, I would also understand if you want to stay at Mac's. He's a great guy, and I think he likes you."

Allison knew the offer of hospitality was sincere. They had shared their belief in God, and Penny, who prayed on a regular basis, was much better than her when it came to faith. Hers felt shallow compared to Penny's and Mac's.

I never even thought to pray about all this before. I never prayed about my move here. Would I have made it if I had? Would I even be tangled up with Jack if I'd prayed about him? Too late now, Allison was just glad she had a praying friend. She needed to start reconnecting with God. Why had she ever quit?

She squeezed Penny's hands. "You are such a good friend. Oh, I am so thankful I met you here. I have my cell phone on silent and with all that's going on, forgot to take it off. That's why I didn't answer. I think I should leave Mac's. He hasn't said I should, but I don't want to impose on him or be a bad influence on Paddy. It's better if I only see him at school.

"Thank you for the offer. I would like to come stay if you're sure it's okay. I...I am afraid to go back to the house in case Jack comes back. He kind of spooked me. And with the police looking for him, as well as those other weird guys, I don't know what to think. Thank you. Maybe I can pay you back someday."

"Not to worry. Bring your stuff over and we'll get some girl time in. Maybe we can figure out what's going on, and how you got into this fix." Penny rose and grabbed the top of the futon sitting at one end of her living room, preparing to flatten it into a bed. Allison helped, then left as her friend headed to her linen closet.

"I don't like it," Mac said as she stood in the kitchen explaining her move.

"I don't want you to leave either!" Paddy added.

"Well, Penny has invited me to stay with her for a while, and I think that would be fun for me, don't you, Paddy? You like to stay overnight with your friends, don't you?" She wanted to avoid spelling out her real reasons in front of him. She appealed to the father with her eyes.

"You understand don't you, Mac? I think it's best."

"Maybe," he responded. "But will you be okay?" His wrinkled brow as he bent his head and searched her face showed his worry for her safety.

"I am sure I will be. We'll leave for school and come home at the same time. It probably won't be for very long. You can come by and visit," she said and wondered where that came from. An unconscious wish spoken aloud?

"Okay, do you want me to come with you to your house to get more things?" Mac crossed his arms and squinted as he studied her.

"Can I come too?" Paddy questioned.

"If you want to," Allison responded. She glanced at the young boy to see the hopeful expression on his face turned toward his father.

"No, Son, I don't think this time. But you can visit Ms. White over at Ms. Parker's place. Won't that be fun? You'll visit two teachers!"

"But, Dad..."

"No, Paddy. I'll be back soon. You stay with Mrs. Thompson. I won't be gone long." Allison watched him turn from the pout forming on Paddy's face and walk over to pick up her bags where she'd placed them and hold the door for her. She felt the magic between them brush her with warmth as she passed by him. Had she made the right decision?

Allison packed more clothes and toiletries into another suitcase back at her rental while Mac stood looking out her kitchen window, almost as if he expected someone to show up. She remembered she had lived there with a body in her backyard and felt jumpy. She was ever so grateful this broad-shouldered man had agreed to accompany her today, even though he didn't seem certain of her innocence in all this.

Mac turned as the woman he couldn't stop thinking about came from her bedroom with a big suitcase. He hurried to relieve her of the burden and as he leaned to grab the handle, her face looked up at him and came dangerously close to his. He trembled with need.

Without thinking he set the suitcase down and put his hands on her shoulders. Bringing her into the circle of his arms seemed so natural. She shuddered as she laid her cheek against his chest. He threaded his fingers through her hair.

"Allison…" Her name escaped on his breath.

She looked up at him and he slowly lowered his lips to hers. The force that brought them together so primal and strong, it coursed through his whole being as a physical yearning.

Her lips were warm, soft, and so sweet. He deepened the kiss and knew the impact in his soul. His body's response that followed alerted him to back off. He pulled away.

Opening his eyes, he saw confusion in hers, and want. He yearned to gather her close and repeat the kiss but knew he shouldn't. It was too soon, too much. And while his heart said she was everything she appeared to be, his mind still held an element of doubt. Who was she and was she real? And was she what God would want for him? Perhaps he was being tested.

He didn't know what to say. Should he apologize, tell her he was coming to care for her, or just ignore it? Her eyes contained questions he couldn't answer.

He grabbed the suitcase. "We'd best get over to Penny's. Don't forget to lock the door here."

Confused, Allison stared after Mac as he headed out to the vehicle. That kiss had turned her insides to molten lava. She'd noted the tremor in Mac's hands. But then he'd turned away as if it was nothing. She didn't understand men. Men seemed to be able to run hot and cold when it came to emotions. She heard the pickup door slam outside and, gritting her teeth, hurried after the big *galoot*. She'd bet *that* was a western term that fit.

CHAPTER TWENTY-TWO

As Penny and Allison arrived back at Penny's place after school the next day, a black car pulled up. Allison froze with fear as she stood on the sidewalk. Was it the mob again?

She let out a breath and loosened her stance. A man in a dark suit and blue shirt unbuttoned at the neck, creating a somewhat casual look, approached her. His blond crewcut and friendly smile had her making a mental comparison between him and the obvious mobsters who'd visited her. He showed her a badge that read FBI. She tensed again.

"Ms. White?" His heavy accent drew the "w" out on his "White," making her name sound like "Ms. Watt." She recognized his heavy New York accent though it was from a different area than where she grew up.

"Yes."

"Awm Agent Grimstone." He held up his badge. "Terrible name for maw line of work, huh?" He held out his hand to her. "Awe need to visit with you for a few minutes. May we go inside?" Another man got out of the car and headed their way.

Allison gave Grimstone her limp hand as a small greeting and glanced at Penny who was poised in the act of unlocking her apartment door. It was convenient that each ground-floor apartment in the building had its own private, outside entrance, making it easier for Allison when she'd moved in with her still-healing ankle.

"Please come in." Penny finished turning the key and walked in, holding the door open.

The small apartment shrank with the addition of the agents. Why more FBI? Hadn't she told everything she knew to the first two?

Grimstone gestured toward the second man. "Maw partner, Agent Gohens."

Grimstone sat on the put-together futon, after inviting the two women to sit in the recliners. Penny's presence didn't seem to bother him. Allison clasped her hands together. Gohens stood with feet apart and arms crossed by the entrance as if guarding her possible escape.

"What do you know about Arnie Augustino?"

Allison's head jerked up. "Augustino? That was his name? I don't! I mean, I don't know anything about him. I didn't even know his last name."

"How did you meet him?"

"Jack, my ex- fiancé, and I, had dinner with Arnie and a woman, Wanda, and another couple one night, in New York. They were friends of Jack's, my fiancé then. He isn't my fiancé now. I told him we were through when he was here, last weekend, and he left." She shifted in her seat and lifted a quivering hand to brush back a strand of hair that had escaped her ponytail. *I must look guilty. Like my students when they've done something wrong. They don't look me in the eye.* She looked back at the detective, forcing herself to make eye contact.

He studied her face with an intensity that made her squirm again.

"I'm not guilty of anything! Don't you believe me?" *Stupid. Why ask that? Now I sound guilty. What has Jack gotten me into?*

"Ms. White, you are innocent until proven guilty."

Allison looked into Grimstone's eyes, wondering why she felt any responsibility in Arnie's death, Jack's running off, being in this mess, involving Mac. She had always led a guilt-ridden life, at fault for something, even when she wasn't. She thought she'd grown out of that old insecurity, but apparently not.

"Nothing. I've done nothing!"

"Good," the agent smiled at her. "I believe that's awll for today. Stay around, and we'll be in touch." He stood. She and Penny rose to their feet also and watched as he strode to the door, opened it, and followed by his partner, walked out without looking back.

She sank down into the recliner again. "Why are they after me? Why four of them? These guys are from New York." She looked at her friend. "I don't have any idea about any of this! Why was Arnie in my backyard? Why is he dead for that matter? And why is Jack hiding? I need my dad." Her cold hands clutched the fabric arms in a vice-like grip as if seeking something solid to hold onto.

"Boy, their accent is so thick, you can cut it with a knife! Yours isn't that bad. Is there more to the story?" Penny asked. "Maybe I can help you figure it out. But you should call your father first. Can he help you?"

"He's a lawyer. It's probably why Jack wanted to marry me, I'm thinking now. Especially after what I heard in the restaurant the night I met Arnie." She frowned. "I have an accent?"

"Yeah, different than the western drawl out here, that's for sure. But talk to your dad, then I want the whole story. I'm your friend. I believe you. You're not a murderer. I'll go fix a sandwich for us."

Allison's dug into her purse for her cell phone.

CHAPTER TWENTY-THREE

Mac, walking beside her, reached for her hand as they walked toward the entrance to the Natrona County International Airport in Casper. His mouth was tightly closed, and he made no eye contact. A tired, defeated feeling hollowed out a place inside her. Their clasped hands had none of the comforting flow of energy she'd experienced in the past.

He had agreed to come with her to meet her father as he flew in from New York. But his emotional support seemed to be nonexistent.

"Thanks for being with me today." She didn't look at him as she said the words, couldn't bear to see more nothingness in his expression. His opinion had come to be so very important to her. Thoughts of Mac continually occupied a corner of her mind and a tiny thrill danced through her heart when she acknowledged them. She longed to see an understanding light in his eyes now, a light that would shine on her with warmth and caring. But it wasn't there.

She trained her eyes back on the jet coming in for a landing. Oh, how she hoped her dad could make sense of this and make her feel safe again. She shivered in the strong Fall breeze. If only it would blow her troubles away as easily as it blew the dust rising and swirling around them.

"Let's go inside and greet him. He'll have to pick up his luggage," she peeked up at the stony-faced man beside her.

"Why don't you go? I'll bring your car. It won't take long. This is a small airport." With that, Mac steered her toward the terminal building's sliding glass door and dropped her hand, heading back to the parking lot. It was the bit of dust in her eye causing a tear to fall, she was sure of it.

"Dad!" Allison's arms were around his neck before he could even drop his briefcase to return the hug. To her dismay, she found herself sobbing into his shoulder.

"Hey, hey, what's going on, Peanut?"

The use of the name he'd called her when she was small caused more of the emotional dam she'd been building in the past few days to crumble and spill tears onto his jacket. Words couldn't stick together through the flow of water from her eyes.

"Mr. White." Mac's voice cut through the waves.

Allison pulled back from her father as she felt his arm reach out behind her to grasp Mac's hand.

"Dr. MacFadden. I'm Grayson White. Thank you for coming with Allison to meet me."

"You're welcome. The luggage carousel is over this way, and I have the car waiting right outside."

He sounded in a hurry to be on the way home. Where was the concerned vet-to-the-rescue she'd met at the dance? She was too needy.

Her dad kept his arm around her as they walked to the carousel. Mac grabbed the suitcase as her dad identified it. Soon they were in Allison's car, Allison beside her dad in the backseat, traveling back to Sage Flats. Belatedly, she wondered if her father was hungry.

"Are you hungry, Dad? They don't feed you on airplanes anymore, do they? We could stop in some little town and get a hot dog or something. I'm sorry I didn't think to ask when we were still in Casper." She kept her face averted, knowing her reddened nose and swollen eyelids from crying made her unattractive to men. Hiding her flaws was a habit, though she knew her dad would never censure her. She turned her head to the window, surreptitiously wiping her nose with the tissue hidden in her hand.

"It's okay, Peanut. I had a good breakfast and it's only mid-afternoon. Lots of days I don't stop for lunch. Would you like to tell me what's been happening since we talked, or wait until we get back to your home?"

"Well," Allison hesitated, wondering where to start since her dad knew most of it already. "Mac knows everything, so I can tell you now. If you're not too tired."

"Never, Honey. Tell me. I need to hear all the details if I'm going to help you."

"I'm so glad you're here. The FBI questioning me is scary. And one said I might need an attorney.

"One of the men at the table in the restaurant in New York—the night I told you about when I heard the women talking in the bathroom about Jack—was Arnie, the man found buried in my backyard. When I talked to you on the phone, I didn't tell you he was Jack's friend. *I* didn't think Jack would murder a *friend*, but now I'm not so sure." Her breath hitched on the word "murder."

"But how and when did his body get in your backyard? Why hadn't you noticed?" Her dad's gaze was penetrating. She withered with her stupidity, shrinking down in her seat.

"I don't know! My backyard is overgrown with grass and weeds. I don't go back there. I *never* go back there! There are probably spiders and snakes in the grass." She shuddered. "Mac discovered the grave. I don't know when it was dug or why Arnie was in it!" A sob escaped.

"It's okay, Honey." Her dad's arm circled her shoulders. "Shh. We'll figure this out. Tell me more."

Allison detailed all the worries crowding her mind—the threats by Arnie's wife, the visit by the Mafia, the questioning by FBI agents, Jack's behaviors, worry about her job, and the safety of herself and her new friends. She told of the kindness of Mac and Penny. Even though she'd shared most of it with her father on the phone already, telling him while having him physically present helped take her anxiety level down a notch.

"But with you here, we can go back to my house." She suddenly remembered she'd never completed her reason for her trip to the hardware store.

CHAPTER TWENTY-FOUR

Allison looked at her dad across the breakfast table. It had been such a comfort and feeling of security to have him with her. She wanted him to get to know Mac. But Mac hadn't even shown the brim of his white hat since he'd brought them home from the airport the day before. Had all her "baggage" been too daunting for him? She closed her eyes and remembered the day he'd charged into her kitchen and lifted her off the floor while Jack had looked on with a sneer. But, maybe he was busy at his clinic this morning.

Things were so complicated. What had happened to the simple plan to move to "small town" Wyoming, and disappear amongst fifth graders and sagebrush? To leave her concerns and past mistakes in New York?

"Honey," her dad began, "I have to go back to New York. I want you to come back with me. I don't want to leave you here. I don't think you're safe. Your mother would feel better if you were at home too.

"I have to do some investigating to find out how that body got in your backyard, why you were thrust in the middle of this and by whom. I will try to locate Jack. He sure fooled your mother and me. We thought he was a straight-up guy.

"If Mafia is involved, you may be in danger. I can find out what the police are doing. I'll contact the FBI. Good to know they are involved. The fact that they sent agents out from New York means something important has happened in the criminal world that might be an advantage to them.

"Since I am personally involved, I'll get one of my associates to help and represent you if it should be needed. Come back with me."

He leaned forward and took the hand she had lying beside her plate into his warm, reassuring grip. He looked into her eyes with the same persuasive focus she'd always caved into as a child when he'd wanted her cooperation.

Yes, she thought. *I want to crawl up into his lap and let him safeguard me.* But then the heady feeling of being on her own which she'd experienced that night at the roundup dance popped into her thoughts. Even though she'd fallen on the dance floor and made a spectacle of herself. The exhilaration of being rescued by a cowboy, or vet masquerading as a doctor, she reminded herself, had been exciting...totally out of her known hemisphere. She'd felt independent, free, and as if she were finding out who she might be when she grew up, besides being a schoolteacher. At twenty-five, she should be feeling mature, self-confident, able to handle any new experience. If she went back to New York with her father, she'd again be the sheltered, naïve city girl, under her parents' wings. Did she want that?

"I..."

A loud knock on the door interrupted her. She pulled her hand from her father's and rose to answer it.

"Wait!" Her father stood up. "Let me open it!"

Allison shrank back, knowing why he said it, but feeling a familiar resentment with his taking charge of things...of her, in her home—the first one she could call her own. Her resentment fled when he unlocked and opened the door, and in walked her guy in the white hat.

"Allison? Are you okay?" Mac searched Allison's face. Her furrowed forehead and troubled eyes had him reaching for her.

Allison's father extended his hand. Mac dropped his arms that hadn't yet made contact with Allison and reached over to shake the hand. "Good morning, Mr. White."

"Call me Grayson, and I hope it's okay if I call you Mac. I hope you can persuade Allison to return to New York with me tomorrow. I don't think she's safe here."

Mac had been saying his morning prayers, including asking his heavenly Father to watch over Allison and keep her safe, when he'd gotten a sudden urge to check on her. He didn't question it, having found his occasional urges usually nudged him in the right direction, especially when they had something to do with what he was praying about. He'd learned to obey even when they went against his self-made decisions, like maybe the wrong decision to leave Allison entirely in the hands of her father and remove his own hands. What did God want him to do? His personal feelings were all over the place.

He looked at Allison. Wide-eyed, she was staring at him with a "little girl lost" look that settled right into his heart. Without thinking, he turned and opened his arms, and she walked right into them. Their difference in height allowed her to always lay her head on his chest just above his heart, as their arms encircled each other.

Mac glanced up to see Grayson White rubbing his chin in a thoughtful manner. Allison backed out of his embrace and turned toward her father.

"I don't want to go back. I don't want to feel sheltered anymore, Daddy. I'm out on my own now. I don't think I'm in danger. I'll stay with Penny again. And the police here are aware of what's happening, they're even suspicious of me so they are keeping a close eye on me. As is the FBI. So everyone is probably watching me and keeping track of me. Mac will watch out for me too. He knows everyone in the community so will know right away if someone strange comes around again. And he's met Jack." Mac nodded his head when she glanced at him.

"I will look after her too, Grayson. I'll keep an eye on things. If she stays, she can continue her job. We need teachers here and Allison is a good one." Mac put a hand on her shoulder.

"I would like her with me where I know she'd be safe." Her dad didn't appear to care for opposition to his statement.

"Dad, I need to grow up and stand on my own two feet. I've been too passive with my life. I like Wyoming. It's wide open, quiet, and the people are great here. I'll be ok. I'll text you or call you every day if you like. I have friends here already who'll look out for me. I won't stay alone."

Heavy silence filled the space among the three as her father studied the two of them. He sighed. "I'll leave tomorrow again then. Get started on my investigation. Get you a lawyer. I have a friend in mind. I'll call and see if I can get an airline ticket. Since it's a school day, can you take me to the airport, Mac?"

"Be glad to. Let me know what time your flight leaves. Here's my card with my phone number."

Allison turned to the dishes in the kitchen sink. A falling tear popped a soap bubble. She hoped her little speech to her father was what she really wanted. Was she ready to be on her own with this? Maybe getting back to class tomorrow would renew her self-confidence.

What if the school board decided she wasn't fit to teach because of her proximity to the situation? Surely the whole community would be wondering about her...maybe even thinking she's guilty of murder and hiding a body in her backyard, even if it wasn't hidden very discreetly.

CHAPTER TWENTY-FIVE

Monday, and the kids were lively, yet thoughts of Arnie's dead body and Jack's visits slithered in between commands of "Let's use our indoor voices," and "Open your books to page 30." Allison shook her head as if she could get rid of the images that incessantly pecked at her mind like persistent woodpeckers. She forced her concentration back to her students.

After school, Allison parked in front of Dave's Hardware Store with renewed determination to get a gun. Maybe he offered lessons too.

"So, you want to buy a gun. You think you need it? Have you ever owned one?" Dave's litany of questions chopped at her bravado.

"No. but I live in the West now, don't I? Doesn't everyone own one? Do you give lessons?" Her voice tone rising with each question, she clamped her lips tight and gripped her purse handle.

"No, we don't give lessons, but there is a place about ten miles out of town that's a sort of free shooting range. All the locals use it to practice their aim. No targets except sagebrush and rocks. It's kind of gotten to look like a war zone. People leave spent shells and pieces of target behind. There's a big red bluff behind the spot so you shouldn't have a bullet zing out over the prairie and hit something...or someone you don't want to. You might want to get a friend to go out there with you. But let's talk guns. Got anything in mind?"

"Uh, what would you recommend?"

She left without one. Too many choices and not enough knowledge muddled her ability to decide, and fed her fright, leaving her feeling helpless and totally clueless about how she should prepare to defend herself...if it ever came to that. She shuddered.

She'd talk to Penny and Mac about it...if Mac was even still interested in her safety. He hadn't texted or called after he took her dad to the airport that morning. His "I'll keep an eye on things" was maybe an empty promise when it came to *her* things. Perhaps she expected too much. She really had minimal experience with men. Jack was the first one she'd ever dated for any length of time.

She remembered her half-brave words to her dad, how she could look after herself and the whole community would watch out for her. She knew she didn't believe all of what she said inside herself...why would so many people be concerned about her welfare...a recent transplant from New York? But she meant to forge new paths, develop new strengths, become her own person in this rugged Wyoming. Enough with the passive, dependent personality she recognized in herself.

She reached her car and watched the lights blink as she pushed a button on the key fob. She gasped when a hand grabbed the door she was pulling to a close as she settled behind the steering wheel.

"What were you doing in Dave's?" The words were harsh and demanding. Terror morphed into anger when she saw the white hat capping the speaker.

"And just what would you care?" she ground out, glaring at his scowling face.

"I said I'd keep an eye on you and give you advice when you said you wanted to own a gun, or have you forgotten? Did that fool Dave sell you one?"

"None of your business. I'm not your responsibility! Just go about your life." She had no idea where her rage came from. She knew fear usually masqueraded as anger and wondered why she was taking it out on Mac. And why was *Mac* angry?

As their eyes locked above the glowering, a stirring in her heart became a lump in her throat, and small rivers ran down her cheeks.

Mac's frown lines softened, and his hand extended toward her. She took it without understanding the force drawing her out of the car and against his chest, into his arms again.

She needed a hanky, or handkerchief as the cowboys called it. Sniffling, she realized one was touching her hand, a large red one rippling through her tears. Embarrassed now, she backed out of the sinewy embrace and blew her nose. Oh, why did she have to cry so easily?

"I'll take it home and wash it."

Warm, rough fingers lifted her chin.

"I genuinely don't want you to have a firearm. They can be dangerous to the user as well as the bad guy. And do you really think you could shoot someone who threatened you? Could you shoot Jack?"

"I...I don't know. But I'm unnerved by all this. I know I told Dad everyone was watching out for me, but no one here has a good reason to look out for me. I'm not a child, although I pretty much lived like one in New York with my parents. I worked and set up my own schedule, but I counted on them to guide me and shield me from anything unpleasant or hard. And I thought Jack would fill that spot when we got married. I'm such a poor judge of character."

For a moment, the muscles in Mac's cheek rippled as he studied her. "Join me for supper over at the café and we'll talk about this. About what might happen. I do want to help. I'm not going to prey on you or take advantage of you. That's not how it works with me.

"The cops can't be everywhere. Our police force is small for this little town. The FBI agents have left. I only want to be your friend and keep our newest teacher safe." He held his elbow up, inviting her to hang on.

She locked the car and imagined locking a pathway to her heart also. Her ex-fiancé scum didn't deserve her leftover feelings from memories of when she'd thought he loved her, and Mac didn't deserve her foolish attraction. He just wanted to keep the "newest teacher safe." Grow up and stop being so emotional, she told herself.

She stumbled on the curb and felt a long arm unfold to circle her waist. Security. She righted herself and stepped away from it, walking into the café with her head high.

"Dr. Mac!" The trim waitress hurried over as they seated themselves. "Your usual?" Her eyes never strayed from his face.

"Is that the chicken fried steak special? Then yes, my usual. Sandy, this is my friend Allison. Would you bring her a menu? She's not as well versed in all the great meals you offer."

The waitress's smile slipped a bit as she eyed Allison. "Need a menu, Hon?"

"Yes, please." The waitress sauntered off with hips swaying.

"Now tell me. Are more scary things happening?"

"Can I tell you when we are alone somewhere? It's not something I want overheard. But it's serious, very serious, and I don't think we should spend time together anymore."

CHAPTER TWENTY-SIX

Allison and Mac sat in his pickup outside Penny's apartment while the flood of words filling the car about the things frightening her spilled out. "You know the Mafia is looking for Jack. And they weren't telling the truth why. Maybe they want to hurt him or...kill him. And you know the FBI doesn't know where he is. And he was *here*! And I thought he seemed scared. And that isn't like him. And now, *Dad* suggested Jack might have killed Arnie! Or at least have put the body in my backyard. And that makes sense as he was parked back there and crawled in my window. I had thought of that when I saw Arnie's body, but wouldn't let myself believe it." She covered her face. Saying it out loud made her own suspicions more real. And if Jack had buried a dead man, then touched her...she closed her eyes as if she could erase the visual memory of his helping her in and out of his car the night he took her home from the restaurant.

"You know everything, you must have had suspicions too. I need you to tell me—what should I do? Where should I go? What if I'm alone somewhere and Jack comes *back*? He wants me with him for some reason. Am I endangering people at the school? And maybe Penny? Am I endangering you? That's why we shouldn't spend any time together. You might be in danger because of me." She grabbed his hands as she turned to him with wide eyes. "You have to leave and not come around me anymore. Maybe I shouldn't be teaching school. I was such a fool to think I could leave my troubles in New York."

"Whoa," Mac responded. "I don't think either of us is in danger. Jack has left. He's the one the Mafia wants, right? To reassure you, if they wanted *you*, you'd be gone by now. You don't know how that body ended up in your yard for sure, and you were gone from New York before all this went down."

"Yes, but you said Wanda accused me of killing Arnie when she called for me at your place! She knows where I'm at. Why is she accusing me? I've never done anything to *her*! Or to Arnie. I'm afraid she's setting me up and someone will believe her and come after me!" Allison's voice pitched higher and louder. She couldn't control the geyser of panic filling her chest.

"Shhh. It's okay. We'll figure this out. We need to tell the police here what's going on in case the FBI hasn't filled them in. I'm not going anywhere. I can take care of myself. Call the school tonight and leave a message that you can't come in tomorrow. That you're sick or something again. We'll go to the police right away in the morning. Make sure you pull the shades on any windows and lock the door after I get you inside the apartment. I believe you're safe but might as well take precautions."

Goosebumps sprouted on her arms as Allison made the rounds of the apartment pulling down shades and turning on a lamp. She wanted Penny home, but it was her bowling night. She'd be alone for a couple of hours yet.

Her eyes roamed the space, fixating on the door. How much of a barrier would it be if a man really wanted to bust through it?

Hastening to the bedroom to slip into sweats, she shrieked when her cell phone rang. "God's Country" played, meaning she didn't know the caller. She'd picked that tune to indicate she'd arrived in a welcome and safe, country place, and it would mean new friends were calling. Penny's name was already added to her phonebook with a different tone, and unless this was Mac, she didn't want this call.

Dread squeezed her heart as she pulled her phone from her purse. Recognizing a New York area code, she let it go to voicemail. After staring at it for several minutes when the chime let her know the message was ready to listen to, she entered her password, getting it wrong the first two times as her mind refused to function normally. She hit the speaker icon.

"We know you overheard us that night at the club," Wanda's nasally Bronx accent identified the voice. "But," a sob and noisy sniffle interrupted, "You didn't have to kill him! He was my only love! We've been together five years! He was my everything." Her voice strengthened to a more aggressive tone. "They've got the goods on you. You won't get away with this."

Allison fumbled to end the call and dropped the phone. "You bitch!" echoed through the room as the small device hit the floor on the accuser's grand finale.

Sinking onto the futon, numb with shock, her body folded into a ball, shoulders hunched, and arms hugging her knees. Only her eyes moved as they darted around the room, seeking reassurance she was by herself within the now-seemingly paper-thin walls.

Two hours later, her body froze when she heard Penny's key in the lock, but then realizing who it had to be, her tears released the mountain of fear holding her hostage. Ashamed of her loss of control, she kept her head buried in her knees. Her stomach hurt as jerking sobs racked her body.

Penny's voice penetrated her harsh weeping. "What happened? Are you okay? What's wrong?" Positioning herself beside her friend, she placed an arm around her. "Tell me, what's going on?"

Allison fought to calm herself. "I had a call, from Wanda, Arnie's wife. She thinks I killed Arnie because of what I heard in the bathroom at the restaurant the night I met her. She's figured out I was in the stall listening to them. But I swear I didn't know who they were then, or that it was my Jack they were talking about! I didn't even think I should take it all seriously at first! I can't kill someone! I've never even killed an animal, let alone another human being! But she might send someone after me. She said, 'They've got the goods on you, and you won't get away with it!' But does she mean the Mafia will be after me or the FBI? She called me a bitch. This is so scary! Maybe I *should* go home to

Daddy. How does she keep finding out where I'm at? Who's watching me and letting her know?"

Her friend was silent for so long, Allison got up to pace. "I'll leave, go back to New York, get out of everybody's hair here for everyone's peace of mind. But it will be so hard to give up my dream of independence...finding myself on a new adventure. I'm beginning to love all the kids here. I thought I'd left any issues with Jack in New York. Stupid me!"

"Wait! Don't make hasty decisions." Penny rose and caught Allison's arms as she marched by.

"What? It's not hasty. Dad asked me to go with him when he left last week! It's been simmering in my mind since then, and I've been fighting it. But with the mafia, the FBI, and Wanda all hounding me, I can't fight it any longer. And I don't want to put you in peril by living with you, or anyone else. Dad's a lawyer, he'll help me out of this and find protection for me if I need it."

"Let's call Dr. Mac. Perhaps he can come up with a solution so you can stay here. You could go live with him. His housekeeper can be a chaperone. I'll call. And we should go talk to the principal at school too—Mattie Gray Cloud. Make sure she's aware of things and still okay with you teaching." Penny paced as she outlined a course of action.

"I never thought of talking to the principal! I've wondered if I might be a danger for the kids!"

"Now, I don't think there'll be a problem," Penny said quickly. "We're a pretty tight community and we take care of our own. When we had a motorcycle gang come into town last year, headed to Sturgis, South Dakota, for the big rally that happens every summer, a bunch of locals came into town too, packing guns. Not causing trouble but ready to respond if the gang did. It's legal to carry here. The bikers ate at the local café and bar and left peacefully, looking over their shoulders as they roared out of town. We'll help you."

"But I'm not really one of you, I've only been here two months, and look at the disruption and notoriety I've brought! And why would you believe me? I look and feel guilty myself!" Allison flopped down on the futon, her legs noodling on her.

Penny pulled her cell phone out of her hip pocket and poked the screen. "Dr. Mac? Hi, are you busy? Can you come over to my place again tonight? We need another brain to pick. Is yours available?"

Mac looked at the hopeful faces of the two women, their eyes searching his, obviously hoping he had some wisdom to share. His only thought was wanting to go to Allison and wrap his arms around her as a shield of safety and comfort. He couldn't understand his lack of objectivity around this one woman who had so recently disturbed his little piece of paradise. Or was it his "peace" of paradise? He almost smiled at his little inner pun.

"Don't you think the school board will be okay with Allison staying on as a teacher while this mess sorts itself out?" Penny asked, bringing Mac's concentration back to the situation.

"Well, we can find out. Let's go talk to Mattie and see where she stands." Facing things sooner, rather than later, might be to Allison's advantage. Or it might bring Allison's crisis to the school's attention. And she'd have to leave, and maybe lose her job. Mac wasn't sure where he stood. His head said let her go back to New York, and his rebellious heart said do what he could to keep her here.

"I'll meet you at the school at 8 AM tomorrow."

CHAPTER TWENTY-SEVEN

"And so, class, I would like you to write five paragraphs giving me some unusual and interesting facts on Alaska. However, include some common ones too, like how and when Alaska came to be included in the United States, who the people are, and how the state is important to us economically."

Allison smiled at the twenty fifth-grade faces of her history class. They had wrangled their way into her heart the past two months, each with a unique personality and need for motivation to learn. She hoped her teaching methods would at least pique an interest in studying history in everyone by the end of the year.

Mattie Gray Cloud had been very understanding and said she would visit with the school board if Allison's position became an issue over the body of Arnie. There were no charges against her, so no change was needed in her status at this point Gray Cloud assured the three when Penny and Mac accompanied Allison to the school the morning after her call from Wanda.

As her credentials from her past teaching jobs stood her in good stead, the principal saw no reason to question Allison's credibility. That did not mean Gray Cloud wouldn't be close by as Allison went through this—still on probation as a newbie. But she could keep her job and tentative independence for now.

"Please, God, let it be forever," Allison's lips had moved with the words as they walked out of the office.

Two weeks had passed with no more alarming incidents and a modicum of security had settled in Allison's heart.

Now, as the final bell rang shrilly through the hallways, ending the day, the principal squeezed into the classroom through the flow of escaping students.

"Ms. White? Would you come with me?"

"Can I gather my materials to take home and lock up first?"

"I'm afraid not. Perhaps you can later."

Perhaps? "What's this all about?"

The female principal's heels clicked loudly and rapidly as they hurried down the hall. "You'll see."

As Mattie opened the door to her office, Allison halted at the sight of the two FBI agents she knew as Grimstone and Gohens standing by the desk, eyes on her and faces of stone.

"Please, come inside," Mattie said.

Terror slid down her body, becoming a physical weakness, and she stiffened herself to remain standing. She struggled to ask the question, "What's going on?"

"Allison White, you are under arrest for the murder of Arnie Augustino."

CHAPTER TWENTY-EIGHT

"Allison, Allison, you can wake up now. Can you hear me?"

A warm, wet washcloth lay soft across her forehead and the awareness coincided with the sound of the voice.

Squinting at the freckled face's eyes searching her eyes, Allison parted dry, sticky lips. "Where am I?"

"You're at the Sage Flats Hospital, Dear. You fell and bumped your head when you fainted. You have a concussion. Do you remember anything about it?"

Scrutinizing the ceiling, which stayed plain white with no hints for her, she answered, "No, can you tell me?" She switched her gaze to the nurse's hazel eyes.

Glancing at the room door as it opened, the freckled nurse said, "Well, we'll let Agent Grimstone refresh your lost memory."

Allison focused on the black-suited man with the silver tie as he came into the room. Her eyes slid to the face above the suit and fear gushed through her like water rushing over a dam. It all came back.

Her head was pounding, and a gray haze shimmered in her peripheral vision. She opened her mouth to better suction enough oxygen to stay conscious. Her parched tongue formed words with no sound at first. Then blinking rapidly, she rasped, "Why?"

"Why what, Ms. White?" The expressionless face of the FBI agent stared down at her. She vaguely noted the false sense of reassurance that the side rails on the bed would keep her safe from him.

Licking her lips, she tried again, forcing sound through vocal cords stiff with fright. "Why am I under arrest? I didn't kill, Arnie."

"We believe you did, Ms. White." The words, hard-edged and delivered in the low baritone of the steely-faced man, sharpened the sudden rhythmic throbbing in her temples.

"But I *didn't* kill him! I told you. I didn't kill him! Oh, why won't you believe me?" She turned her head back and forth on the pillow, tears seeping out of her eyes and zigzagging a path into her ears. Her lungs hurt as she fought to breathe between her sobs. Her head ached.

"You will have a chance to prove that in a court of law, Ms. White. An attorney has been hired to defend you by a friend of yours I understand. As soon as you are able, we will take you back to New York. Meanwhile, I will be stationed right by your door. You are going nowhere until you are discharged. You have a good rest until we leave." The man turned and straight-backed, exited, his shoes clicking rhythmically on the tiled floor.

Allison glanced at the woman in blue scrubs standing silently in the background throughout the exchange. Wearing a name tag labeled "Sally RN," she approached, supporting Allison's head with one hand while whipping her pillow out, turning it over, and stuffing it back under her head with the other hand. The actions didn't feel gentle, and the nurse's lips were compressed. *Guilty as charged* read the unspoken message.

"You get some rest, sounds like you have a rough time coming. Let me know if you need something." The nurse disappeared through the doorway without looking back.

Night brought a darkness so cavernous, Allison thought she'd never rise to light again.

Mac sat at his kitchen table, physically vibrating with anxious energy and nerves, yet so exhausted, he felt he'd just completed a marathon. One leg jumped up and down and his fingers drummed the laminated surface. He'd been told he couldn't see Allison at the hospital, that she'd been arrested and was under guard by the FBI. For a moment, the shock of that news, whispered to him by Alice, a nurse he knew, made him dizzy. He'd walked out of the hospital not knowing what to think, what to do.

Why am I interested, even more than interested, in someone who might have murdered? And how could I misjudge her so? Although, let's face it, what experience do I have with big-city women? New York even? I've been duped. Fooled. Small-town idiot. And why did I pay a retainer for a lawyer? Her dad has money. He can do it.

He couldn't erase the memory of her face when he'd seen her at Mattie's office. She'd looked so relieved when the principal had assured her about her job continuing and that her problems would, no doubt, be solved soon. And genuine. Not a big-city fake. She'd looked like someone he could believe in, and someone for whom he could let his interest continue to grow. And it *had* grown. He'd taken her to church with him and Paddy twice since then. She'd seemed genuine in her worship.

"Well, Stupid," he spoke softly to himself, "live and learn." Perhaps tomorrow his heart would feel whole and unencumbered. Or maybe tomorrow it would still feel heavy and struggle to keep its rhythm.

His cell phone vibrated in his shirt pocket. He looked at the time—midnight. He realized he'd been sitting at the table rethinking the situation with Allison for over two hours, convincing himself he'd done all he could for her, and it was over for them if it even started. Well, now he could think about something else.

He recognized the number on the screen as from his friend Brad, a rancher 60 miles away with a thousand head of cattle. The rancher also raised prized bulls for sale. If a bull was sick, he'd need to get his mind off personal issues to treat a possibly miserable and angry 2000-pound animal. Fatigue battled with relief at the interruption as he left a note for Regina Thompson and headed to his truck.

Handcuffed, face hot with shame, Allison kept her eyes trained on the floor tile as Agent Grimstone guided her through the loading gate and onto the plane at Natrona County International Airport. She was glad the place was small and the passengers few in the late afternoon.

Not mentally ready to leave her hospital bed and face whatever ordeal awaited, she'd nonetheless been discharged to the custody of the agent. No familiar faces had appeared, leading her to believe no one had been notified of her departure or status. They'd only kept her 24 hours. She still had a slight headache.

The recollection of meeting her father at the airport a few weeks earlier, with Mac beside her, surfaced and drove the current pain and sense of betrayal by whoever was responsible for this deep into her marrow. Someday she would find out who did this and make them sorry. If she wasn't locked away for life in a federal prison. Just the thought had her stumbling and the silent, straight-postured man beside her gripping her upper arm hard enough to leave bruises.

"Keep walking now, Ms. White. No trying to get away or delay us. It won't work."

Grinding her teeth and pressing her lips together, she concentrated only on not collapsing as she walked up the boarding ramp, lifting her head high. She had to develop some backbone and prove she was innocent. Yet she felt like a campfire marshmallow, singed and crisp on the outside, enabling it to keep its shape, and melting on the inside—her bravado a thin veneer that would collapse into mush at any moment.

She didn't have to see the actual jail cell in New York to imagine the horror of being locked up. She sat wooden and tense, feeling like she was being transported to the guillotine.

She felt exposed as they changed planes at Denver and again in Chicago. *How can criminals live with this constant sensation of being a beacon of guilt? Do they truly have no conscience, so they don't feel it?*

Her thoughts whirled and traveled multiple paths at once. All the people chaotically swarming, passing, and buzzing with conversation at the airports, seemed perfectly in tune with the chaos inside her.

By the time they landed and transported her to FBI headquarters in New York, it was as if her body was asleep. Her mind rolled in on itself. *I'm a zombie. A body with no soul.* A vacuum sucked her weightless corpse from place to place in a preposterous world, leaving only her fingerprints and mugshot behind on pieces of paper.

Then a door opened, and life returned. Her father was there.

"Daddy!" She had no sense of getting up and falling into his arms, but as if a computer monitor that had gone dark started working again, she was back in reality with all the horror it now held for her. And except for the arms around her holding her together, she would have exploded into tiny bits from the tremendous pressure in her chest.

"It's okay, Peanut. We'll figure this out. Everyone knows you wouldn't murder anyone or even be friends with anyone who could. It's okay, it's okay." The words unleashed a cloud burst of tears from Allison with no seeming end.

Finally, having nothing left to fill her tear ducts, she lifted her face, but her dry, gritty eyes refused to bring clarity to her father's image. She hung her head and was so grateful when he put his arm around her shoulders and turned her toward the door.

"You're free for now, Peanut. I posted your bail. Let's go home."

I'm not free. Will I ever be again? Worry and trepidation weighted every footstep away from the courthouse.

CHAPTER TWENTY-NINE

She'd been home six weeks, or out on bail, she reminded herself, home in a holding pattern, like a doomed jet circling the sky waiting for a landing place that never opens. She had nowhere to go in life but down, down to a life without freedom, pride, or purpose. How could she fight this situation when she would most likely be fighting the mob?

Fear and anger became the guards that kept her prisoner in her parents' home. Fear that she was being watched by mobsters and the FBI. Unbecoming bursts of anger popped out at her parents over trivial things—why were they out of orange juice when she needed some now? She even felt anger at people who drove through their neighborhood. Were they spying on her?

She'd had a few good friends before she dated Jack, pretty much ignoring them when focusing on him, and now they ignored her. Her attempts at calling them ended with having to leave messages which brought no callbacks from them.

She hadn't heard from Mac. That bothered her most of all. Thank goodness Penny wrote to her weekly. But she was a walking time bomb, ready to explode at the slightest provocation and shatter everyone around her, including herself.

She clung to the promises of her daddy that she'd soon be free. She'd regressed to thinking of him in that term again instead of "father." She wanted to believe his assurance that this would be made right. She was innocent and no one could find her guilty of murdering someone. Oh, how she wanted to believe that.

"Honey?" Her mother's voice floated up the curved staircase to her bedroom.

Allison gazed at the doorway from her vantage point beside her dressing table. She didn't know how long she'd been sitting there staring at the floor, unable to propel herself down to the kitchen for breakfast. She'd slept the night through from exhaustion and the temporary feeling of security by being at her parents'. But now, the sun shone on a day full of dread that filled her chest with heaviness and stole her energy. Looking at her watch, she marked another half hour of existence borne. She couldn't even summon a prayer about her circumstances.

"What, Mom?" With great effort, she worked to make her voice loud enough to be heard downstairs to the foyer where she knew her mother stood.

"You have mail, Sweetheart. From a veterinary clinic in Sage Flats. Did you have a pet there, Dear?"

A trickle of life flowed back into her veins. Her head lifted and she prayed with hope. *Thank you, Lord, for a letter from Mac. Don't let him give up on me. Please.*

Her lower limbs like the soft linguine they'd had for supper last evening, Allison descended the stairs clinging to the railing and praying she wouldn't stumble. Her hand eagerly reached for the envelope bearing the Sage Flats Veterinary logo in the return address.

A bench by the foyer table beckoned her and she sank to the padded seat, focusing on the unopened letter in her hand.

"Well, pita rolls and coffee are in the dining area when you're done reading your letter."

Relieved her mom left, she ran a fingernail under the corner of the envelope flap in slow motion, forcing an opening. The folded paper inside tantalized her yet thickened the trepidation of what she might read as she unfolded the note written on Sage Flats Veterinary Clinic stationery.

Dear Allison,

You haven't heard from me for quite a while, but I think of you all the time. I pray for you.

How are things going? Have they caught the murderer? I googled for information but haven't found anything.

Are you ok? I have a lot of questions and no answers. But I have been asking around here at home. Trying to find clues. So far, a lady who lives a couple blocks from your house remembers your ex-fiancé's Porsche going by several times back when he first showed up at your place. She remembers seeing it turn in behind your house in the middle of the day when you would've still been at school, then couldn't see anything after that.

I saw Dave at the café and he mentioned a guy driving a Porsche stopped in and bought a shovel one day. So, I guess that tells us who put Arnie in your backyard. I've let the police here know. They said they'll make sure the FBI knows.

Have your dad call me sometime. Maybe we can get a lead on more information. I hope the lawyer I hired for you is helping. He was recommended by your dad. Your dad said he'd pay for him, but I want to help.

Your friend,

Mac

Her vision blurred. She heard her mom return and felt reassuring hands rest on her shoulders.

"Oh, Mom. At least he signed it 'Friend.'"

"Who did, Honey? Is that from your veterinarian friend? Is that the man your father met and who offered to pay for legal defense for you? Your father was impressed with him. Said he seemed to really care about you."

Allison nodded, jarring loose a sob and rivulets of tears to drip off her chin. "Dr. Ian MacFadden. Everyone there calls him Dr. Mac. I thought he was a real doctor when I first met him at the dance.

"He took me to the hospital when I sprained my ankle. We were just starting a friendship when Jack showed up saying he wanted to be engaged again. Jack said all kinds of things he didn't mean, Mom. I've been so blind."

"We were too. We thought he was a great guy with a good business. We had no idea what he was into. Oh, I'm so sorry we encouraged you with him. Do you think this Dr. Mac is different?"

"I know he is. I want to be able to go back. I like Sage Flats. People are real there. And life is not so complicated, or maybe it is, but it's genuinely complicated with caring about each other and making a living. It's not an artificial feeling." She looked into her mother's face for understanding.

"Well, Dear, when this is sorted out, you can go back. We can help."

"If I can go on teaching. Oh, things are such a mess." Allison mopped a stupid tear off her face with her shirt collar.

"We'll just see what your defense lawyer can do. Let's not think about it right now. Come have a cup of coffee with me. We'll pray first about this whole fiasco. God will get you cleared and the real murderer behind bars."

That sounded reasonable, but Allison knew in the past, her mother sometimes used prayer time to tell *God* what would happen and how "they" would accomplish it. She hoped that's how it worked this time. She knew her mother would have ideas.

Christmas came, and Allison went through the motions without engaging much of her heart. She received a beautiful, gold-embossed card showing Baby Jesus in a brown manger, and signed "Your friend, Mac," which caused mixed feelings of sorrow and joy. At least he still thought of her.

The usual gift-giving and attendance at a candle-lit Christmas Eve service failed to lift her spirits, even though she felt a presence that comforted her in between bouts of panic. Many short prayers moved her lips daily.

And then, just after New Years, she received news she'd been waiting for. The truth had been discovered at last. She would attend a trial in the near future, but it wouldn't be hers.

CHAPTER THIRTY

The temperature raised goosebumps, and the sky dripped icy rain on their faces and pathway as Allison and her parents walked into the courtroom eight weeks later, sitting near the back, wanting to draw as little attention as possible. With ice-cold hands gripping her father's arm, Allison knew God had listened when her mother told Him who should be convicted of murder in this case. This was their second time in the courtroom—the first for Wanda's sentencing, and now for Jack's.

They rose from the hard courtroom bench to the bailiff's call.

"All rise! The court of the Seventh Judicial Court, Criminal Division, is now in session. The Honorable Judge Whitney Hammer is presiding."

She struggled with the exertion of standing. Her fifteen-pound weight loss during the past three months in New York didn't seem to make the rising easier for Allison. Even her usual designer high heels felt loose. She gripped the back of the bench in front of her.

She now knew what she was made of. Between her arrest and the dates of these trials, which was a remarkably short time according to her lawyer but seemed a lifetime to her, she had found an anchor in herself. She was made of stern stuff.

Through depositions, prayers, and support from her attorney and family, she had persevered in proving her innocence. She still needed to work on not being angry, but a therapist she had seen a few times told her that was righteous anger and was healthier than the anxiety attacks that plagued her for a while.

The time spent agonizing over her arrest also birthed some personal revelations. She was an adult, temporarily hiding under her parents' wings again, it was true, but she had moved to Wyoming, successfully done her job until Jack derailed her, and now possessed more of an idea what a true and honorable man should look like. And if the one she knew wasn't interested anymore, she would live through it.

The jury filed in, many glancing at her as they did so. Now, what did that mean? She wasn't the one being sentenced here. Were there friends of Jack's on the jury? Or were they just curious to get a glance at someone who'd been engaged to him?

Wanda had been the killer of Arnie all along. She had hired Jack to dispose of the body and tried to put the blame on Allison.

How could a woman kill her husband? Kill anyone? All because of jealousy. He'd had a girlfriend on the side. It hadn't been a true Mafia killing as they'd feared.

The trials had taken two weeks, one week for Jack and one for Wanda. Quick convictions happened in both cases, brought on by the overwhelming evidence that Jack had left in his wake: showing up in Sage Flats driving a flashy car, hiding it in Allison's backyard and leaving tire tracks behind, buying a shovel at Dave's Hardware, not being able to hide the DNA from Arnie's body scrunched into the trunk of his car, and a host of other things, providing an easy trail for authorities, causing them to take their focus off of Allison and withdraw the charges.

Wanda should have hired someone smarter, but then Allison should have chosen someone smarter as her first love. She thought the mob's defense team would have fought harder, but perhaps they were just as glad to be rid of Jack as she was.

Jack, with an ego bigger than his brain, and trying to shield Wanda after she told him he was the man she wanted, spread the lie that Arnie was a victim of the mob. Hence the mob's interest in finding him. He'd wanted a cover when he asked to become re-engaged to Allison and change his name to hers. Now he went to prison along with Wanda for his part in being an accessory to the murder. Going to prison probably saved his life from what the crime society might have done to him. She wondered if he'd even be safe now, in prison.

She need not be concerned about him anymore, yet she was sad for him and what might happen. They'd had some good and tender moments when his affection for her had felt genuine. She experienced a moment of grief for what might have been.

Back at their house, Allison collapsed on her parents' French settee and sank her face into the throw she grabbed from its corner. It was over.

The tension and emotional burdens still weighing her down poured out of her eyes, and nose too, it seemed. She wiped it all on her mother's afghan, a totally gross and immature action, but right now she didn't care.

Her mother and father had hurried into the bedroom and closed the door as soon as they all returned from the trial. Why weren't they out here comforting her? Then again, she didn't want anyone to see how weak she still felt sometimes, not even her parents.

She had to admit that as much as crying released tension over the ordeal of the murder and trial, tension about her relationship with Mac remained. She hadn't heard from him for five weeks, one day, and six hours, not that she kept close track. She told herself she was glad he hadn't come to the trial of Jack, even though she'd penned a short letter telling him the date and that she had already been cleared. Why did life always bring bitter and sweet together? Sorrow and victory? Should she go back to Wyoming?

Allison lifted her reddened, wet, and mucus-smeared face from the throw as the sound of murmured voices came down the hall. Her mother came toward her, straightening her tailored suit jacket in sync with compressing her lips in a "I don't like it and we'll see" expression. A familiar look used often during Allison's childhood when her parents didn't agree on what to do with her.

She looked up at their watery images and focused on her dad's face which seemed much more forgiving. "What?"

Her mother spoke through stiff lips as she pulled a tissue from her sleeve and handed it to Allison, "Do you want to go back to Wyoming?"

Did she? Yes, if her teaching position was still open to her. Not so sure, if Mac wanted nothing to do with her. She realized her heart was more involved than she'd thought. She'd never allowed herself to acknowledge how deep her feelings ran for her new home and the guy in the white hat while being distracted when accused of murder.

She'd put many of her feelings on hold during the last three months, the only way she knew to survive emotionally. Now, emotions from A to Z flooded and overwhelmed her, making her heart thud as if too burdened to keep beating. What should she do?

Allison's eyes darted between her parents' faces, trying to decipher what she should answer, then realized she was reverting to what she now called her "PEW" ways—Prior to Escaping to Wyoming.

She'd changed, left the shelter of her childhood home, made decisions independently of her parents, and while trouble had followed her there, she'd found strength and stamina she hadn't known she possessed because of it.

She'd taken a risk in fleeing to Wyoming, then a big test had come her way when she was charged with murder, and she'd begun to rely on God and those who loved her for emotional survival. But she had grown in self-confidence. She remembered the Bible verse in Second Timothy she'd clung to the past few months: "For God hath not given us the spirit of fear; but of power, and of love, and of a sound mind."

Could she survive Wyoming with God's help even if Mac didn't see her as anything more than a friend? His last letter, coming on the heels of his Christmas card, had been full of life in Sage Flats, at the veterinary clinic, how much Paddy missed her at school and a reminder that he prayed for her. No declaration of feelings other than friendship.

Penny had written weekly, regaling her with stories from school, and always signing the letters "with love." Mac signed, "Your friend." Could she live with that?

"Yes!" She looked hard at her mother's face, noting a tear glistening on her cheek. "I know you might think I shouldn't. But I want to.

It's a good place for me. Remember, you agreed you'd help me go back. And I hope you can come and visit me. I won't be running away from something this time when I go there, I'll be running to something. I've made friends and started learning who I am. I hope you can understand."

"We do, Honey," her dad answered. "Come here." He held open the arm that didn't already encircle her mother. She moved in for the group hug. She'd miss them so much but needed to leave. Even if nothing further developed between her and Mac.

"I'll call the airlines. Maybe Penny can drive to Casper to pick me up this weekend. Mac has my car stored at his clinic." Her words came faster as she turned toward the stairs to run up to her room to pack. Scenarios of what would happen when she met Mac again began running nonstop through her mind.

Allison's spaghetti legs reappeared as she hurried through the chute between airplane and terminal in Casper. Penny had assured her she'd be there to pick her up and bring her back to Sage Flats. Twin rivers of excitement and apprehension coursed through her veins.

Passing through the last checkpoint into the terminal's public waiting room, she searched for Penny's face and found Mac's.

"Wha-a-a, what happened to Penny? Is she sick? Did you have to take her place?" Her voice weakened just a bit as she neared Mac and looked up at his face.

"You came back." His intense gaze seemed to hold longing. "I wasn't sure you would."

"Is it okay with you, that I came back? Are we still friends?"

Immediately Allison chided herself. She didn't need his okay, she was in charge of what she did and why she did things now. Wasn't she? She was fishing, wanting to know his reaction to her coming back.

"It's more than okay. Do you...can we...would you be more than my friend?" His hands on her shoulders shook. Her knees were knocking together.

Swallowing, she nodded. "Do you want me to be?"

"I wanted to meet you. I wanted to be here to welcome you back." His voice gained strength as the words rolled out like the tumbleweeds that rolled across the streets in Sage Flats. "I've missed you. Paddy has too. I mean..." He hesitated, moistening his lips and Allison noticed his Adam's apple bobbing up and down, "I think I might be falling in love with you, but I had to know you could choose to come back to Sage Flats again. Could you like it here enough to stay? And like me enough to let me court you? Give you some time back here again, to make sure you want to stay?"

Mac's face was way too high for her. She shrugged out of the backpack and as it thudded on the floor and as people maneuvered around them, she jumped up and wrapped her jean-clad legs around Mac's waist, her arms around his neck, and met his surprised look by closing in for a kiss that was quickly returned as passionately as it was given.

Suddenly realizing how they must look to the other passengers, even though a quick glance showed no one paid attention as they hurried to the luggage carousel at the other end of the terminal, she dropped her feet back to the floor. Keeping her eyes on his, she answered, "I like you very much. I might even fall in love with *you*. You can court me. I'm staying. Let's go home."

CHAPTER THIRTY-ONE

The leftover winter after she'd returned to Sage Flats had been a hard one. Blowing snow and two long episodes of below-zero temperatures had only increased Allison's pride in herself. Rumors and half-truths about her absence and situation floating around the community had also infused her students with curiosity, which they weren't shy about sharing. She told them just enough, she hoped, to assuage their fears about her being their teacher, and their need to know about her arrest and innocence. Maybe she could instill in them the goal to be honest and to not be afraid when needing to overcome obstacles in life.

She'd been so thankful for the school family and community which had welcomed her back, once they knew the whole story, and supported her in her attempts to become a part of life in this sometimes harsh, but beautiful location. The unfriendly weather, and the red buttes guarding the flat valley, made her feel isolated yet safe while she healed and lost the fear and sense of violation that Jack had caused by reappearing in her life.

But Mac had backed off in his pursuit of her. Had she horrified him with her declaration at the airport? They dated once a week. Unable to stay in the house where a pile of dirt in the backyard brought her a memory of Arnie lying there, silent and dead, he'd helped her move into the apartment building Penny lived in.

She saw Paddy every school day and was in love with this small version of his dad. He was thoughtful, and polite, and took his studies seriously.

Mac had taken her to supper, and to basketball games at the school—casual, friendly things, except the time he got called out to a ranch at the beginning of a date and she'd tagged along. She'd seen her first calf born. She'd been ecstatic and felt she'd witnessed a miracle. It showed determination to stand only minutes after it'd been born. *I need that determination,* she'd told herself. And resolved to develop it as she learned to live in the West.

By the beginning of May, a permanent relationship with Mac didn't seem any closer. Maybe she'd read his interest wrongly. Perhaps he'd changed his mind as he got to know her better. Maybe he'd decided they should stay casual. Their goodnight kisses sizzled with heat. But she knew she was as inexperienced in healthy relationships as that newborn calf had been in walking.

Should she look for someone different? She knew where her heart lay, but no sense "beating a dead horse" as she'd overheard a retired rancher say one morning when she walked past the usual group of men in the local restaurant having their daily coffee. While not knowing for sure what the rancher had meant, the saying seemed to fit her situation. Not that Mac was a dead horse. She chuckled in spite of her dreary thoughts.

It was springtime when love was supposed to be in the air. She'd received interested looks from some single ranch men. Maybe she should give a look back next time. Let this strong feeling she had for Mac and his son settle down a bit. If she could. Her next year's teaching contract was already signed. She wasn't going anywhere.

As if God agreed with her, the next Saturday morning as she sat in the Sage Flats Café, her usual Saturday morning spot for reading the local weekly paper over a sweet roll and coffee, a tall man about her age, wearing jeans, a tucked-in blue western shirt, and a grey wide-brimmed hat, sauntered over to her table.

"Can I join you, ma'am?"

"Sure. Have we met?"

"I'm Clint Saunders. I know you're Allison White, one of our newest schoolteachers, and one of the most interesting new people our town has had in centuries, I'd guess!"

Knowing what brought that last statement on, she was speechless and wondering how to reply and if this was God's answer to her earlier reflection when a gruff voice spoke up.

"Clint! Good to see you! Haven't seen you around for a while. Excuse us. Allison and I have some important business to discuss over breakfast. But let's you and I have coffee the next time you make it off the ranch! Take care, now."

Clint took the hint and faded into the background as Allison, open-mouthed, watched Mac slide into the booth beside her instead of across from her.

"Important business?"

"Yeah. Will you marry me?"

Allison swallowed, her mouth suddenly lacking spit. She reached for her water glass and took a sip.

"Why?"

Mac's gaze slipped from her face to her hands. "Because I love you and want you to wear this." He pulled a small box out of his shirt pocket and opened it to reveal a simple gold ring supporting a large sparkling diamond.

Speechless, Allison's eyes darted from the ring to his face and back. He was proposing to her in a restaurant? She glanced around, at least ten pairs of eyes were watching them, including Clint's.

"I know it's not the ideal spot to propose, and I meant to take you for a drive up into the mountains to some beautiful spot, but I saw Clint here and thought I better just do it now. Don't go looking for someone else. I know I'm slow, but I was afraid you were going to leave again and not come back. I had to be sure you plan to stay here.

"I've loved you for a long time. I'm sorry I've been so cautious. I have Paddy to consider too, but last night he asked me why I hadn't asked you to marry me. He said he wants you for his mom. Guess that was the last push that I needed toward doing this. Then seeing Clint trying to make time with you panicked me into thinking I might lose you if I wait any longer. I've had the ring for a few months. So, will you?"

It was the longest speech she'd ever gotten from him. He usually was a man of few words. The café in Sage Flats was the equivalent of a fine steakhouse in New York she supposed, so receiving a proposal there maybe wasn't so far out she guessed, but at breakfast?

She started to giggle and couldn't stop. Other patrons in the restaurant began giggling too, probably overhearing, or deciphering what was happening by his body language and the way he'd latched onto her hands before producing the ring sparkling in the café lights. But when she looked at Mac, she sobered up. His ears were red and his hand holding the ring twitched. So, she followed another impulse, after grabbing the ring and sliding it on her own finger, she threw her arms around him, and yelled, "Finally! Yes!" The kiss that followed turned the crowd's giggles into clapping.

"Let's get out of here." Mac's low-pitched voice growled as he ended the kiss.

"Better get a preacher!" The yell followed them out into the May sunshine.

"July?"

Mac nodded. "The sooner the better. I want you as my wife. I love you."

"I will love you and Paddy forever. Let's go tell him."

She couldn't help the thrill rippling through her whole being as she circled her arms around his neck and looked up into eyes that slowly closed as his lips lowered to hers.

Yippee ki-yay! She'd have to learn to yodel. She was going to live in the West! And she'd gotten the good guy in the white hat.

Acknowledgements

Special thanks to my writing friends in the Casper Writers critique group who helped refine and shape this story. Also, a big heap of gratitude to my daughters, Shannon Bodin, and Stephanie Voss, for editing and encouraging me. It is with gratitude I acknowledge they are smarter than I am.

Thanks also to my wonderful granddaughter, Elizabeth Bankert, who read my story in its infancy and encouraged me.

And praise and thanks to God who laid the story on my heart.

Don't miss out!

Visit the website below and you can sign up to receive emails whenever Neva Bodin publishes a new book. There's no charge and no obligation.

https://books2read.com/r/B-A-ECPJ-XJPNC

BOOKS 2 READ

Connecting independent readers to independent writers.

About the Author

Neva Bodin writes fiction and non-fiction. Publishing credits include a devotional, two childrens' books, a western novel, short stories, newsletters, poetry, and freelance articles. Find her at nevabodin.org. A new middle/grade young adult fiction is coming in 2024.

Neva is a member of Casper Writers, Kingdom Creatives; Wyoming Writers Inc., American Christian Fiction Writers, WYO Poets, Daughters of the American Revolution, and Art On The Go. Find her on Facebook at Neva Bodin author/writer, Twitter@NevaBodin1 or you can contact her at https://nevabodin.org or nevab@atwy.net

Read more at https://nevabodin.org.

* 9 7 9 8 2 2 3 2 9 5 1 5 0 *